THE HOUSE OF SCORTA

by Laurent Gaudé

Translated from the French
by Stephen Sartarelli and Sophie Hawkes

THE HOUSE OF SCORTA

by Laurent Gaudé

Translated from the French
by Stephen Sartarelli and Sophie Hawkes

Lawson Library
A division of MacAdam/Cage Publishing
155 Sansome Street, Suite 550
San Francisco, CA 94104
www.macadamcage.com

Library of Congress Cataloging-in-Publication Data

\

Gaudé, Laurent.
  [Soleil des Scorta. English]
  The house of Scorta / by Laurent Gaudé ; translated from the
French by Stephen Sartarelli and Sophie Hawkes.
      p. cm.
  ISBN 1-59692-159-5 (hardcover : alk. paper)
  I. Sartarelli, Stephen, 1954- II. Hawkes, Sophie. III. Title.
  PQ2667.A873S6513 2006
  843'.92—dc22

                                                        200502445

Paperback edition: January 2007
ISBN 10: 1-59692-055-6
ISBN 13: 978-1-59692-055-2

Manufactured in the United States of America
10 9 8 7 6 5 4 3 2 1

Book design by Dorothy Carico Smith.

For Elio
A bit of the sun of these lands
flows in your veins.
May it light up your eyes.

Camminiamo una sera sul fianco di un colle,
In silenzio. Nell'ombra del tardo crepuscolo
Mio cugino è un gigante vestito di bianco
Che si muove pacato, abbronzato nel volto,
Taciturno. Tacere è la nostra virtù.
Qualche nostro antenato dev'essere ben solo
—un grand'uomo tra idioti o un povero folle—
per insegnare ai suoi tanto silenzio.

We're walking one evening on the flank of a hill
in silence. In the shadows of dusk
my cousin's a giant dressed all in white,
moving serenely, face bronzed by the sun,
not speaking. We have a talent for silence.
Some ancestor of ours must have been quite a loner —
a great man among fools or a crazy old bum —
to have taught his descendants such silence.

—CESARE PAVESE,
from "I mari del Sud"
("South Seas"), in *Lavorare stanca*;
English translation by Geoffrey Brock (Copper Canyon Press).

I

THE HOT STONES OF DESTINY

*T*he heat of the sun seemed to split the earth open. Not a breath of wind rustled the olive trees. Nothing moved. The scent of the hills had vanished. The rocks crackled with heat. August weighed down on the Gargano massif* with the self-assurance of an overlord. It was impossible to believe that rain had ever fallen on these lands, that water had once irrigated the fields and quenched the olive groves. Impossible to believe that any animal or plant could have ever found sustenance under this arid sky. It was two o'clock in the afternoon, and the earth was condemned to burn.

A donkey trudged along a dusty path. Resigned, it followed every curve in the road. Nothing could impede its progress. Not the burning air it breathed, not the jagged stones mangling its hooves. On it went. Its rider was like a shade condemned to an ancient torment. Dazed with heat, the man didn't move. He left it up to his mount to lead them both to the end of that road. The animal performed its task with a blind force of will. Slowly, step by step, lacking the strength ever to quicken its pace, the donkey ate up the miles. The rider was muttering, his words evaporating in the heat. "Nothing can stop me… The sun can kill all the lizards in these hills, but I'll hang on. I've been waiting too long… The earth can hiss and my hair catch fire, but I'm on my way, and I won't stop till I've reached the end."

Thus the hours went by, in a furnace that consumed all color. At last, behind a bend, the sea came into view. "Here we are, at the ends of the earth," the man thought. "I've been dreaming of this moment for fifteen years."

The sea lay motionless, like a puddle, as if its only purpose were to reflect the sun's power. The road had not passed through any villages or intersected any other roads, but only plunged further and further into the land. The sudden appearance of that immobile sea, sparkling with heat, made it clear that the path led nowhere. Yet the donkey went on at the same slow, decisive pace, ready to plunge into the water if his master asked him to. The rider didn't move. He felt dizzy. Perhaps he had made a mistake. There was only a maze of hills and sea, as far as the eye could see. "I took the wrong road," he thought. "I should already be able to see the town. Unless it moved away. That must be it. It must have sensed I was coming and moved, into the sea, so that I couldn't get to it. I'll dive into the waves if I have to, but I won't give in. I'll go on till I've reached the end. I want my revenge."

The donkey reached the top of what seemed like the last hill on earth. That was when they saw Montepuccio. The man smiled. He could take in the whole town at a glance. A small, white town, with houses huddled together high on a promontory overlooking the deep calm of the sea. This human presence in so barren a landscape must have seemed comical to the donkey, but the animal did not laugh and kept on walking.

When they'd reached the town's first houses, the man said under his breath, "If a single one of them tries to prevent me from passing, I'll crush him with my fist." He carefully studied every street corner, but he was soon reassured. He had made the right decision. At that hour of the afternoon, the village was dead. The streets were deserted, the shutters closed. Even the dogs had vanished. It was siesta time, and were the earth itself to tremble, not a soul would venture outside. There was a legend in town that told of how one day, at this hour, a man returning late from the fields crossed the central square. By the time he'd reached the shade of the houses, the sun had driven him mad. As though its rays had burnt his brain. Everyone in Montepuccio believed this story. The square was small, but to cross it at this time of day was to welcome certain death.

The donkey and his rider went slowly up what, at the time, in 1875, was still the Via Nuova, but would later become the Corso Garibaldi. The rider clearly knew where he was going. Nobody saw him. He didn't even come across any of the scrawny cats that usually prowl for rubbish in the gutters. He made no attempt to put his donkey in the shade or to sit himself down on a bench. On he went, obstinate and terrifying.

"Nothing has changed here," he muttered. "Same lousy streets. Same filthy houses."

That was when Father Zampanelli saw him. The

village priest, whom everyone called don Giorgio, had forgotten his prayer book in the little plot of land next to the church that he used as a kitchen garden. He'd worked there for two hours that morning, and it had just dawned on him that he'd left the book on the wooden chair near the tool shed. He'd gone outside the way one does during a storm, body hunched, eyes squinting, determined to be as quick as possible to avoid exposing his mortal flesh to the heat that drives people mad. That was when he saw the donkey and its rider making their way up the Via Nuova. Don Giorgio paused for a moment and made the sign of the cross. Then he ran back behind the heavy wooden doors of his church to protect himself from the sun. Surprisingly, he didn't think to raise the alarm or call out to the stranger to find out who he was or what he wanted (travelers were a rare sight, and don Giorgio knew everyone in town by first name). In fact, once back in his cell, he gave it no further thought. He lay down and sank into the dreamless sleep of summer siestas. He had crossed himself at the sight of the rider as if to dispel an apparition. Don Giorgio had not recognized Luciano Mascalzone. How could he? The man looked nothing like before. He was about forty years old, but had the hollow cheeks of an old man.

Luciano Mascalzone rode down the narrow streets of the old, sleeping village. "It took a while, but I came back. I'm here. None of you know it yet, because you're sleeping. I'm riding past your houses, under your windows. You

suspect nothing. I'm here, and I've come to get my due."
He ambled along until his donkey came to a sudden
stop—as if the old beast had always known that this was
where it was supposed to go, where its struggle against
the sun's fire would end. It stopped right in front of the
Biscotti house and didn't move. The man hopped to the
ground with a strange agility and knocked on the door.
"Here I am again," he thought. "Fifteen years, gone just
like that." An infinity seemed to pass. Luciano was about
to knock a second time when the door slowly opened. A
woman of about forty stood before him. In her dressing
gown. She stared at him a long time, saying nothing. Her
face bore no expression. No fear, no joy, no surprise. She
looked straight into his eyes as if to gauge what was
about to happen. Luciano didn't move. He seemed to be
waiting for a sign from the woman, a gesture, a wrinkling
of the brow. He waited and waited, his body stiffening. "If
she moves to shut the door," he thought, "if she recoils
even a little, I'm going to pounce, kick in the door, and
rape her." He didn't take his eyes off her. He was looking
for the slightest sign to break the silence. "She's even more
beautiful than I'd imagined. I won't die for nothing
today." He could make out her body under the dressing
gown, and this aroused a violent hunger in him. She said
nothing. She'd recognized the man standing before her,
but his presence here, on her doorstep, was an enigma she
didn't even try to comprehend. She simply let the past
resurface in her memory. Luciano Mascalzone. It was certainly him. After fifteen years. She studied him, feeling
neither hatred nor love. She already belonged to him.

There was no fighting it. She belonged to him. Because, after fifteen years, he'd come back and knocked at her door. It didn't matter what he asked of her. She would give. She would consent right there on her doorstep. She would consent to anything.

To break the silence and stillness around them, she took her hand off the doorknob. This simple gesture was enough for Luciano. He could now read in her face that she was not afraid, and he could do with her what he wished. He went inside with a light step, as if not wanting to leave any scent in the air.

A dusty, dirty man stepped into the Biscotti household, at an hour when lizards dream they are fish, and the stones have nothing to say about it.

Luciano entered the Biscotti home. It would cost him his life. He knew this. He knew that when he came back out, people would be in the streets again, life would be back in full swing with its laws and its battles, and he would have to pay. He knew they would recognize him. And kill him. Coming back to this village, entering this house, meant death. He'd thought about all this. He'd chosen to come at the crushing hour when the sun blinds even the cats, for he knew that if the streets had not been deserted, he would never have made it as far as the main square. He knew all this, but did not flinch at his certain demise. He entered the house.

It took a moment for his eyes to adjust to the shadows. She had her back to him. He followed her down a corridor that seemed endless. They entered a small room. There wasn't a sound. The coolness of the walls felt like a caress to him. He took her in his arms. She said nothing as he undressed her. When he saw her naked before him, he could not help but whisper, "Filomena…" A shudder ran through her whole body. He paid no mind. He had all he wanted. He was doing what he had vowed to do. He was living out a scene he'd imagined a thousand times. Fifteen years in prison, thinking only of this. He had always believed that when he finally undressed this woman, he would experience a thrill greater than any physical joy. The thrill of vengeance. But he'd been wrong. There was no vengeance. There were only the two heavy breasts he held in the palms of his hands. There was only the scent of a woman, heady and warm, enveloping him whole. He had so wished for this moment that he now plunged into it headlong, losing himself, forgetting the rest of the world. Forgetting the sun, the revenge, the dark gaze of the village.

When he took her between the cool sheets of the great bed, she sighed like a virgin, a smile of astonishment and pleasure on her lips, and surrendered herself without a struggle.

All his life, Luciano Mascalzone had been what the people of the region, spitting on the ground, called "a bandit." He lived on poaching, plunder, and highway robbery. He may have even killed a few poor souls along the roads of the Gargano, but this was not known for certain. People told many stories that could not be confirmed. One thing, however, was certain: He had embraced *la mala vita*,* and was a man to keep away from.

At the height of his glory — the peak of his career as a scoundrel — Luciano Mascalzone came often to Montepuccio. He was not a native, but he liked the town and spent the better part of his time there. It was here that he first saw Filomena Biscotti. The girl, from a modest but respectable family, became a veritable obsession, but he knew that his reputation prevented him from entertaining any hope of ever making her his own. So he began desiring her the way scoundrels desire women. To possess her, if only for one night. The idea made his eyes sparkle in the late-afternoon light. Yet fate denied him this brutal pleasure. One ignominious morning, five *carabinieri** nabbed him at the inn where he was staying and hauled him away. He was sentenced to fifteen years in prison. Montepuccio forgot him, happy to be rid of this good-for-nothing who ogled their daughters.

In prison, Luciano Mascalzone had all the time he

needed to think about his life. He had devoted himself to petty thievery. What had he accomplished? Nothing. What memories of his past exploits were worth reliving in his prison cell? None. A life had gone by, empty, with nothing at stake. He'd aspired to nothing, and also failed at nothing, since he'd undertaken nothing. Little by little, in the vast expanse of boredom that had been his existence, his desire for Filomena Biscotti began to seem like the only island, the only thing that redeemed the rest. When he had followed her in the streets, trembling, he'd felt so alive he could suffocate. It made up for everything else. And so he had vowed that when he got out, he would sate this brutal lust, the only one he'd ever known. Whatever the price. He would possess Filomena Biscotti and die. Nothing else mattered. Nothing.

*L*uciano Mascalzone came out of Filomena Biscotti's house without having exchanged a single word with her. They had fallen asleep side by side, fatigued by lovemaking. He slept better than he had for a long time. An untroubled sleep. A deep slaking of the flesh, a rich man's siesta, free of care.

He found his donkey outside the door, still coated with the dust of the journey. At that moment, he knew that the countdown had begun. He was heading to his death without hesitation. The heat had abated. The town had come back to life. Outside the doors of the neighboring houses, little old women dressed in black sat in rickety chairs, chatting in low voices, commenting on the incongruous presence of that donkey, trying to guess who its owner might be. Luciano's sudden appearance stunned the old women into silence. He smiled to himself. Everything was as he'd imagined it. "These fools of Montepuccio haven't changed," he thought. "What do they think? That I'm afraid of them? That I'm going to try and get away from them? I no longer fear anyone. They will kill me today, but that's not enough to frighten me. I've come too far for that. I'm untouchable. Can't they understand that? I'm far out of reach of the blows they will surely deal me. I have known pleasure. In that woman's arms. And it's better that it all end right here, because from now on life will be as dull and sad as an empty bottle." At this point he thought of a final provocation to defy the prying stares of the neighborhood women and show them he feared nothing. He ostentatiously buttoned his fly in front of the door. Then he remounted his donkey and headed back the way he'd come. Behind him he heard the old women pipe up again, louder than before. Word was out and beginning to spread, from house to house, terrace to balcony, broadcast by those old, toothless mouths. The buzz grew behind him. He passed through the central square of Montepuccio again. The café tables were out. Men here and there were conversing. They all fell silent as he passed. But the voices behind him only grew louder. Who was he? Where'd he come from? Then a few of them recognized him. Luciano Mascalzone. "Yes, that's me all right," he thought to himself as he passed before their incredulous faces. "Don't waste your energy staring at me like that. It's me, you can be sure of it. Do what you're burning to do, or let me pass, but don't keep looking at me like cows. I'm walking among you. I'm not trying to flee. You are flies. Big, ugly flies. I brush you away with the back of my hand." Luciano rode down the Via Nuova, a silent crowd following behind him. The men of Montepuccio had left their outdoor café tables while the women stationed themselves on their balconies and called down to him, "Luciano Mascalzone! Is that really you? You son of a bitch, you've got balls to come back here." "Luciano! Lift up your head, you swine, so I can see if it's really you." He didn't answer. He stared at the horizon, sullen, without quickening his pace. "The women will shout," he thought, "and the men will strike. I know all this." The mob grew more insistent, some twenty men now hard on his heels. And all along the Via Nuova, the women continued to cry out at Luciano, clutching their children between their legs, crossing themselves as he passed. In front of the church, where don Giorgio had spotted him a few hours earlier, a voice louder than the rest rang out: "Today's the day you die, Mascalzone!" Only then did he turn his head, allowing the whole village to see the horrific smile of defiance on his lips. It chilled them all. That smile told them that he knew, and that he despised them more than anything. That he'd gotten what he'd come for and would take his pleasure to the grave. A few children, frightened by the wayfarer's grimace, started crying. And all at once, in a single voice, the mothers let fly their pious injunction, "He's the devil!"

Finally he reached the edge of town. A few yards away stood the last house. Beyond it lay only the long road of stones and olive trees disappearing into the hills.

A group of men who had appeared from nowhere blocked his path, armed with shovels and pickaxes, their faces hard. Luciano Mascalzone halted his donkey. A long silence ensued. Nobody moved. "So this is where I'm going to die. In front of the last house in Montepuccio. Who among them will be the first to come at me?" He felt a long sigh run down his donkey's flanks and, in response, patted the animal's shoulder. "Are these hicks going to remember at least to give my mount some water after they've finished with me?" He resumed his position, staring at the group of men. The women in the distance had fallen silent. Nobody dared make a move. An acrid odor reached his nostrils, the last he would ever smell. The powerful scent of dried tomatoes. Across all the balconies, the women had laid out broad planks of wood, on which the quartered tomatoes were drying. Burnt by the sun, they shriveled like insects as the hours passed, emitting a sour, nauseating smell. "The tomatoes drying on the balconies will live longer than I."

Suddenly, a stone struck the back of his head. He hadn't the strength to turn around. He struggled to stay upright in the saddle. "So," he had time to think, "that's how they're going to kill me. Stoned to death like an excommunicate." A second stone caught him in the temple, and this time the force of the blow made him reel. He fell into the dust, feet tangling in the stirrup. Blood poured into his eyes. He heard shouting. The men were heating up, each one picking up a stone. They all wanted to strike him. A dense hail of rocks pummeled his body. He felt the hot stones of the countryside bruise his flesh, each blow burning with sun and spreading the dry smell of the hills. His shirt was soaked with warm, thick blood. "I'm down. I won't resist. Go on, strike me. You won't kill anything inside me that isn't already dead. Strike me. I have no strength left. The blood is flowing out of me. Who will throw the last stone?" Strangely, the last stone never came. He thought for a moment that the men, in their cruelty, wanted to prolong his agony. But he was wrong. The village priest had come running and now stood between the men and their prey. He called them monsters and commanded them to desist. Luciano then felt him kneeling at his side. The man's breath blew in his ear. "Here I am, my son, here I am. Hang on. Don Giorgio will look after you." The stoning did not resume. Luciano Mascalzone wanted to push the priest away so the Montepuccians could finish what they'd started, but he hadn't the strength. Didn't the priest know intervention was useless? That it only dragged out his dying moments? Let them stone him with rage and savagery. Let them trample him and be done with him. This is what he wanted to say to don Giorgio, but no sound came out of his throat.

Had the priest of Montepuccio not come between the mob and their victim, Luciano Mascalzone would have died a happy man. With a smile on his lips. Like a conqueror flush with victory, cut down in combat. But he lived a little too long — his life bled out of him too slowly, giving him time to hear what he should never have heard.

The villagers had gathered round his body and, unable to complete their slaughter, began insulting him. Luciano could still hear their voices; they sounded like the last cries of the world. "I guess you won't be wanting to come round here anymore." "We told you, Luciano, today's the day you die." Then came the final injunction:

"Immacolata is the last woman you'll ever rape, you son of a whore." The earth shook under Luciano's depleted body. His mind reeled behind his closed eyelids. Immacolata? Why did they say Immacolata? Who was she? The woman he made love to was Filomena. Immacolata. Filomena. Images from a time long gone merged with the predatory laughter of the mob surrounding him. He saw it all again, and he understood. As the men around him continued jeering, he thought:

"I almost died a happy man… If not for a few seconds, at most. A few seconds too many… I felt the hot stones strike my body, and it felt good… It was how I thought it would be. Blood flowing. Life escaping. And me smiling to the very end, taunting them… It almost happened, but now I'll never know that satisfaction. Life tripped me up one last time… I can hear them laughing all around me. The men of Montepuccio are laughing. The earth drinking up my blood is laughing. The donkey and the dogs are laughing. 'Look at Luciano Mascalzone. He thought he was taking Filomena and deflowered her sister instead. Look at Luciano Mascalzone, who thought he would die in triumph. Look at him lying there in the dust, grimacing like a clown…' Fate has made a fool of me. The sun is laughing at my mistake… My life is a failure. My death is a failure… I am Luciano Mascalzone and I spit on fate, which makes a mockery of men."

The woman Luciano had made love to was indeed Immacolata. Filomena Biscotti had died of a pulmonary embolism not long after Mascalzone's arrest. She was survived by her younger sister, Immacolata, who moved into the family home, the only remaining bearer of the Biscotti name. Time passed, fifteen years of imprisonment. Little by little, Immacolata began to resemble her sister. She had the face that Filomena might have had if she'd been allowed to age. Immacolata never married. She felt as if life had lost interest in her and she would never experience anything more thrilling than the changing of the seasons. In her years of boredom, she often thought back on the man who had courted her sister when she herself was still a child, and it was always with a kind of quiver of pleasure. He was terrifying. His roguish smile haunted her. The memory of him made her drunk with excitement.

Fifteen years later, when she opened the door and saw that man standing before her, asking for nothing, everything seemed clear. She had no choice but to submit to the blind force of destiny. The scoundrel was right in front of her, within her reach. Later, in the bedroom, when, at the sight of her nude body, he whispered her sister's name, she paled. She suddenly understood that he thought she was Filomena. She hesitated a moment. Should she resist him? Point out his mistake? She hadn't the slightest desire to do so. There he stood before her. If taking her for her sister would bring him greater pleasure, she would grant him this luxury. There was no lie in it. She gave in to everything he wanted, without complication. Simply to be, for once in her life, a man's woman.

Don Giorgio had begun to administer last rites to the dying man. But Luciano could no longer hear him. He was doubled up with rage.

"I am Luciano Mascalzone and I am dying in ridicule. My whole life for this bad joke. But it doesn't matter. Filomena or Immacolata, it makes no difference. I am satisfied. Can anyone understand that? Fifteen years I thought of that woman. Fifteen years I dreamed of her embrace and the comfort it would bring me. The minute I got out, I did what I had to do. I went to that house and made love to the woman I found there. Fifteen years, thinking only of that. Fate decided to play a trick on me, but who can fight that? It's not in my power to reverse the course of rivers or put out the stars in the sky. I am only a man. I did all a man can do. I went all the way there, knocked on that door, and made love to the woman who opened it… I am only a man. If fate wants to make a fool of me, I can do nothing about it… I am Luciano Mascalzone and I'm sinking into death, far from the noisy world sniggering over my body…"

He died before the village priest had finished praying. He would have laughed if he had known, before dying, what would come of this day.

Immacolata Biscotti became pregnant. The poor woman would give birth to a son. Thus the Mascalzone line was born. From a blunder. A misunderstanding. From a scoundrel of a father, murdered two hours after the embrace, and an old maid who gave herself to a man for the first time. A family was born. From a man who'd made a mistake and a woman who'd played along with the lie because her knees were clattering with desire.

A family was born of this day of burning sunlight, because destiny felt like toying with people the way cats, using the tips of their paws, sometimes do with injured birds.

The wind is blowing. It flattens the dry grass and makes the rocks whistle. It's a hot wind carrying the sounds of the village and the smells of the sea. I am an old woman. My body creaks like the windblown trees. I am burdened by fatigue and the wind is blowing. Let me lean on you to keep from tottering. Kindly give me your arm. You are a man in your prime. I feel it in your body's calm strength. Clinging to you, I won't give in to exhaustion. The wind whistles in our ears and carries away some of my words. You can hardly hear what I'm saying. Don't let it bother you. I prefer it this way. Let the wind bear away a little of what I'm saying. It's easier for me. I'm not used to speaking. I am a Scorta. My brothers and I were the children of the Mute, and the whole town of Montepuccio used to call us "the silent ones."

You are surprised to hear me speak. It's the first time I've spoken in such a long time. You've been in Montepuccio for twenty years, maybe more, and you've always seen me deep in silence. You thought, like all of Montepuccio, that I had slipped into the icy waters of old age and would never return. Then this morning I appeared and asked for a word with you, and you gave a start. It was as if a dog or the front of a house had begun speaking. You didn't think it was possible. That's why you agreed to meet with me. You want to *know what old Carmela has to say. You want to know why I had you come here, at night. You give me your arm and I lead you down this little earthen path. We have passed the church on our left. As we turn our backs to the village, your curiosity grows. I thank you for your curiosity, don Salvatore. It helps me not to change my mind.*

I'll tell you why I've started speaking again. It's because yesterday I began to go mad. Don't laugh. Why are you laughing? You think that someone can't be lucid enough to know she's going mad, if she really is going mad? You're wrong. On his deathbed, my father said, "I'm dying," and he died. I'm going mad. It began yesterday, and now my days are numbered. Yesterday I thought back on my life, as I often do, and I couldn't remember the name of a man I once knew rather well. I've thought of him almost every day for the past sixty years. Yesterday his name escaped me. For two seconds, my memory became a vast white desert. It didn't last long. Then the name resurfaced. Korni. That was the man's name. Korni. I found it again, but if I could forget his name for even a second, it means my mind has cracked and soon everything will slip away. I know it. That's why I came to you this morning. I must speak before everything is lost. That's why I brought you this gift. It's something I want you to keep. I will tell you about it. I will tell you its story. I want you to hang it in the nave of the church, among the ex-votos. It has to do with Korni. It will look good hanging on the wall of your church. I can't keep it at home. I risk waking up one morning, having forgotten the story behind it and the person I intended it for. I want you to keep it in your church, and when my granddaughter Anna is old enough, you must give it to her. I will be dead. Or senile. You must do this. It will be as if I'm speaking to her across the years. Look. Here it is. It's a little piece of wood I had cut, sanded and varnished. In the middle I had them put this old ticket for the Naples to New York line and, under the ticket, a copper medallion engraved with the words: "In memory of Korni. Who guided us through the streets of New York." I'm entrusting it to you. Don't forget. It's for Anna.

I'm going to talk now, don Salvatore, but there's one last thing I must do. I brought some cigarettes for you. I like the smell of tobacco. Smoke, I beg you. The wind will blow the swirls of smoke to the cemetery. My dear departed love the smell of cigarettes. Smoke, don Salvatore. It will do us both good. Smoke a cigarette for the Scortas.

I'm afraid to speak. The air is warm and the sky hangs low so it can listen to us. I will tell you everything. The wind will carry my words away. Let me imagine that I'm speaking to the wind, and that you can barely hear me.

II

ROCCO'S CURSE

*I*mmacolata never recovered from the birth. It was as if all her spinster's strength had been drained by this exertion of the flesh. A birth was too great an event for this hapless soul, whom life had accustomed to the unbroken calm of empty days. Her body succumbed in the days following the delivery. She grew thinner before everyone's eyes, staying in bed all day, casting fearful glances at the cradle of an infant she didn't know what to do with. She had only enough time to name the newborn child: Rocco. That was all. The idea of being a good or bad mother did not trouble her in the least. Things were much simpler than that. A creature lay beside her, squirming in its diapers, a creature that was all demands, and to whose infinite appetite she didn't know how to respond. The simplest thing was to die — and die she did, one dark September day.

Don Giorgio was called in and kept vigil over the spinster's body all night, as was the custom. Neighborhood women offered to wash and dress the body. Little Rocco was put in the next room and the night was spent in prayer and somnolence. At dawn, when four young men arrived to carry the body away—she was so thin that two would have sufficed, but don Giorgio, for the sake of appearances, had insisted—the women keeping watch approached Father Zampanelli and one of them asked:

"So, Father, are you going to do it?"

Don Giorgio did not understand.

"Am I going to do what?" he asked.

"You know what I mean, Father."

"What are you talking about?" the priest asked impatiently.

"Put the child down. . . are you going to do it?"

The priest was speechless. The old woman, emboldened by his silence, explained that the people in town thought this was the best thing to do. This was the child of a scoundrel. His mother had just died. It was certainly a sign that the Lord was punishing their unnatural union. The best thing was to kill the child, who, in any case, had entered life through the wrong door. But it was not a question of revenge. That was why they had all thought of don Giorgio. His hands were pure. He would simply be giving back to the Lord this little monster who did not belong here. The old woman explained this in all innocence. Don Giorgio was livid. His anger got the better of him. He rushed to the town square, screaming.

"You pack of heathens! The fact that your minds could think of such a heinous thing shows that you have the devil in you! Immacolata's son is a child of God. More than any of you! A child of God, do you hear me? May you rot in Hell if you touch a single hair on his head! You say you are Christians, but you're animals! You deserve for me to leave you to your squalor and God's retribution. This child is under my protection, do you hear? Whoever dares so much as touch this child will have to answer to the wrath of God. This whole village stinks of filth and ignorance. Go back to your fields. Sweat like dogs, since that's all you know how to do. And thank God for a little rain from time to time, since even that is more than you deserve."

When he had finished addressing the stunned inhabitants of Montepuccio, don Giorgio went to fetch the child. That same day he took him to San Giocondo, the closest village, a bit to the north, on the coast. The two towns had always been enemies. Rival gangs fought legendary battles. The fishermen had regular confrontations on the water, cutting each other's nets or stealing the day's catch. He entrusted the child to a fisherman and his wife and returned to his parish. When a poor soul inquired one Sunday, on the town square, what he had done with the child, the priest answered:

"What do you care, you brute? You were ready to sacrifice him and now you're concerned? I brought him to the people of San Giocondo, who are better than you are."

For a whole month, don Giorgio refused to perform his functions. There was no Mass, Communion, or confession. "I'll do my duties the day there are Christians in this town," he said.

Time passed and don Giorgio's wrath subsided. The people of Montepuccio, as sheepish as schoolchildren caught red-handed, crowded around the doors of the church every day. The village was waiting, heads hanging. When All Soul's Day arrived, the priest threw open the doors of the church, and, for the first time in a long while, the bells rang out. "I'm not about to punish the dead just because their descendants are cretins," grumbled don Giorgio. And Mass was said.

occo grew up and became a man. He had a new name—a combination of his father's surname and that of the fisherman and his wife who had taken him in—a name that was soon etched in every mind in the Gargano: Rocco Scorta Mascalzone. While his father had been a good-for-nothing scoundrel who lived on petty plunder, Rocco was a genuine brigand. He didn't return to Montepuccio until he was old enough to sow terror. He attacked the peasants in the fields. Poached livestock. Killed burghers on the roads when they lost their way. He pillaged farms and robbed fishermen and merchants. Several *carabinieri* were sent after him, but were later found by the roadside, a bullet in the skull, pants down, or flung like dolls over the prickly pears. He was violent and insatiable. It was rumored that he had at least twenty women. When his reputation had been made and he ruled the whole region like a lord over his people, he returned to Montepuccio like a man without shame, his head held high. The town had not changed in twenty years. Everything seemed fated to remain forever the same in Montepuccio. It was the same little cluster of houses huddled together. Long winding staircases led down to the sea. There were a thousand possible paths to take through the maze of narrow streets. Old men came and went from the port, climbing up and down the steep staircases, slow as mules pacing themselves in the sun, while groups of children scampered tirelessly up and down the steps. The village looked out on the sea. The façade of the church faced the waves. Year after year, the wind and sun polished the marble streets smooth.

Rocco moved to the upper reaches of town. He appropriated a vast, almost inaccessible plot of land, and had a large, handsome farmstead built there. Rocco Scorta Mascalzone had become a rich man. To those who sometimes begged him to leave the townsfolk in peace and go fleece people in the neighboring areas, he always said the same thing: "Shut up, swine! I am your punishment."

One winter, he paid a visit to don Giorgio. He was flanked by two men with sinister faces and a young woman with a timid gaze. The men were carrying pistols and rifles. Rocco called for the priest, and when don Giorgio appeared, he asked him to marry him to the girl. Don Giorgio did as he was told. When, in the middle of the ceremony, the priest asked the young woman's name, Rocco smiled awkwardly and murmured, "I don't know, Father." And as the priest stood there open-mouthed, wondering to himself if he might be sanctifying an abduction by this marriage, Rocco added: "She's a deaf-mute."

"No surname?" don Giorgio insisted.

"It doesn't matter," answered Rocco, "soon she'll be a Scorta Mascalzone."

The priest continued the ceremony, disturbed by the idea that he might be committing a grievous sin for which he would have to answer to the Lord. But he blessed the union and ended up emitting a deep "amen," the way one says "It's in God's hands" while throwing the dice onto the gaming table.

As the little group was about to climb back into their saddles and disappear, don Giorgio summoned his courage and hailed the young bridegroom.

"Rocco," he said, "I'd like to speak to you. Stay a bit."

There was a long silence. Rocco gestured to his two witnesses to leave without him and to take his wife with them. By now, don Giorgio had regained a sense of equilibrium. Something about the young man intrigued him, and he sensed that he could speak to him. The brigand who had terrorized the whole region had shown a kind of piety towards him, raw but genuine.

"You and I both know," began Father Zampanelli, "how you make your living. The whole land is filled with the tales of your crimes. Men turn pale at the sight of you, and women cross themselves at the mere mention of your name. You sow fear everywhere you go. Why do you terrorize the people of Montepuccio, Rocco?"

"I'm crazy, Father," answered the young man.

"Crazy?"

"Yes, a poor, crazy bastard. You know better than anyone. Born of a dead man and an old woman. God has made a mockery me."

"God does not mock his creatures, my son."

"He made me all wrong, Father. You don't say so because you're a man of the Church, but you think so, like everyone else. I'm crazy, I really am. An animal that should never have been born."

"You're intelligent. You could find other ways to command people's respect."

"I'm rich, Father. Richer than any of the fools in Montepuccio, and they respect me for it. They can't help themselves. They're afraid of me, but that's not really it. Deep down, it's not fear they feel, but envy and respect. Because I'm rich. That's all they think about, money. And I have more than all of them put together."

"You have all this money because you stole it from them."

"You want to ask me to leave your miserable clods of Montepuccio in peace, but you don't know how to do it, because you can't think of any good reasons to convince me. And you're right, Father. There is no reason for me to leave them in peace. They were ready to kill a child. I'm their punishment. It's as simple as that."

"Then I should have let them," retorted the priest, tormented by the idea. "If you steal from them and kill them today, it's as if I did it myself. I didn't save your life for this."

"Don't tell me what to do, Father."

"I'm telling you what the Lord wants you to do."

"Let Him punish me if my life is an affront to Him. Let Him rid Montepuccio of me."

"Rocco—"

"The scourges, don Giorgio. Remember the scourges

and ask the Lord why He ravages the earth with fires and droughts. I am a plague, Father. Nothing more. A cloud of locusts. An earthquake, an epidemic. Everything is topsy turvy. I am crazy. Raving mad. I am malaria. And famine. Ask the Lord. That's what I am. And I will run my course."

Rocco fell silent, mounted his horse and disappeared. That same night, in the privacy of his cell, Father Zampanelli questioned the Lord with all the power of his faith. He wanted to know if he had been right to save the child. He implored Him in his prayers, but was answered only by the silence of the heavens.

In Montepuccio, the legend of Rocco Scorta Mascalzone continued to grow. People said that he had chosen a deaf-mute for a wife—a deaf-mute who wasn't even beautiful—to satisfy his animal desires. So she couldn't cry out when he beat and raped her. And they said that he had chosen this poor creature to make sure that she would hear nothing of his plots, tell nothing of what she knew. Yes, a deaf-mute, to make sure she would never betray him. The man, no question, was the devil himself.

But they also had to acknowledge that, since the day of his marriage, Rocco hadn't touched so much as a hair on the Montepuccians' heads. He had extended his activities deeper into Apulian territory. Montepuccio began to live in peace again, now proud to house such a celebrity. Don Giorgio did not fail to thank God for this return of calm, which he took for the Almighty's answer to his humble prayers.

occo gave the Mute three children: Domenico, Giuseppe and Carmela. The people of Montepuccio hardly ever saw Rocco anymore. He was always on the road, trying to expand his sphere of operations. Whenever he came home to his farm, it was always at night, and one would see candles lighting up the windows. There would be laughter and the sounds of feasting. This would go on for a few days, then all would fall silent again. Rocco never went into town. On several occasions, news of his death or capture would begin to circulate, then the birth of another child would give the lie to such rumors. Rocco was still very much alive. The proof was that the Mute would come into town to shop, and the children would chase one another through the narrow old streets. Rocco was still there, but like a shadow. Sometimes strangers would pass through the village without saying a word, leading columns of mules bearing crates and merchandise. All this wealth flowed toward the great silent property at the top of the hill and accumulated there. Rocco was still there, to be sure, since he was channeling the convoys of stolen goods up to his domain.

As for the Scorta children, they spent most of their time in town, but were condemned to a sort of polite quarantine. People spoke to them as little as possible. The village children were told not to play with them. Time and again, the mothers of Montepuccio would say to their young, "Don't play with those children." And when an innocent child asked why, the reply was always "Because they're Mascalzones." Eventually, the three little children tacitly accepted this state of affairs. They had noticed that whenever a village child would approach them wanting to play, a woman would appear out of nowhere, slap him, and pull him away by the arm, screaming, "Miserable wretch, what did I tell you?" And the unhappy child would run off in tears. For this reason they only played amongst themselves.

The only child who joined their little group was named Raffaele, but everyone called him by his nickname, Faelucc'.* He was the only son of one of the poorest fishing families in Montepuccio. Raffaele had made friends with the Scortas and never left their side, even though his parents forbade it. Every evening when he came home, his father would ask him who he had been with, and every evening the child would repeat, "With my friends." So every evening the father would give him a thrashing and curse the heavens for having given him such a cretin for a son. When the father wasn't around, it was the mother who asked him the ritual question, and she would hit him even harder. Raffaele held out for a month, taking his nightly beating. But the boy had a big heart, and it seemed unthinkable to him to spend his days in any other way than with his friends. After a month, his parents got tired of beating him and stopped asking questions. They had written off their son, concluding they could expect nothing from such an off-spring. From that moment on, his mother treated him like a good-for-nothing. At mealtime she would say, "Pass the bread, ruffian," and she would say it without smiling, without mockery, as a simple matter of fact. The child was a lost cause, and it was better to imagine that he wasn't really her son anymore.

One day in February, 1928, Rocco showed up at the market. He came accompanied by the Mute and his three children, dressed in their Sunday best. This appearance dumbfounded the village. No one had seen him for such a long time. He was now a man over fifty. Still strong, he wore a handsome, greying beard that hid his hollow cheeks. His gaze hadn't changed and still betrayed, at moments, something feverish. He was dressed nobly and elegantly. He spent all day in the village, going from one café to the next, accepting the gifts people offered him, listening to the requests people made of him. He was calm, and his scorn for Montepuccio seemed to have vanished. There was Rocco, strolling from one merchant's stand to the next—and everyone agreed that a man like that would, after all, make a good mayor.

The day ended quickly. A light, chill rain fell on the cobblestones of the Corso.* The Scorta Mascalzone family went back up to their domain—leaving the townsfolk behind to comment endlessly on this unexpected visit. When night fell, the rain grew heavier. It was cold now, and the sea was rough. The waves could be heard crashing all along the cliffs.

Don Giorgio had dined on potato soup. He, too,

had aged. His back was bowed. The work he loved most—hoeing his patch of earth, fixing things up in his church, all the physical tasks in which he found a sense of peace—were now denied him. He had lost a lot of weight. As if death, before coming to get people, needed to make them lighter. He was an old man, but his parishioners were still devoted to him, body and soul. Not one of them would have taken the news of a replacement for Father Zampanelli without spitting on the ground.

Somebody knocked on the door of the church. Don Giorgio started. At first he thought he had heard wrong—perhaps it was the sound of the rain—but the rapping grew more insistent. He rushed out of bed, thinking someone needed last rites.

Before him stood Rocco Scorta, drenched from head to toe. Don Giorgio didn't move, but only stared at the man, taking stock of how the years had passed and changed his features. He'd recognized him, but he wanted to observe the work of time the way one carefully observes the work of a goldsmith.

"Father," Rocco said at last.

"Come in, come in," answered Don Giorgio. "What brings you here?"

Rocco looked into the eyes of the old priest and with a soft but firm voice, answered, "I've come to confess."

Thus began, in the church of Montepuccio, the face-off between don Giorgio and Rocco Scorta Mascalzone, fifty years after the former had saved the latter's life. They had not seen each other since the priest had performed the marriage. The night was not long enough to contain all that these two men had to say to each other.

"Out of the question," replied don Giorgio.

"Father. . ."

"No."

"Father," Rocco repeated with determination, "after you and I have spoken, I shall go back home, lie down, and die. Believe me. I know what I'm saying. Don't ask me why. That's the way it is. My time has come. I feel it. As I stand here before you, I want you to listen to me. You will hear me out because you are a servant of God and cannot take the place of God."

Don Giorgio was astounded by the wilfulness and calm emanating from the man before him. He had no choice but to comply. Rocco knelt in the darkness of the church and recited an Our Father. He then raised his head and began to speak. He told him everything. Every one of his crimes. Every one of his misdeeds. Sparing no detail. He had killed. He had pillaged. He had taken another man's wife. He had lived by terror and the gun. His life had known nothing else. Only theft and and violence. In the darkness don Giorgio could not see the man's features but let his voice fill his ears, absorbing the long litany of sins and crimes flowing forth from Rocco's mouth. He had to hear it all. Rocco Scorta Mascalzone ran down the list of his crimes for hours on end. When he had finished, the priest felt dizzy. Silence had returned. Don Giorgio didn't know what to say. What could he do, after everything he had heard? His hands trembled.

"I have heard you out, my son," he finally murmured. "I never thought that I would live to hear tell of such a nightmare. You came to me. I gave you my attention. It is not within my power to refuse it to any of God's creatures. But I cannot absolve you. You shall present yourself to God, my son, and submit to His wrath."

"I am a man," replied Rocco. Don Giorgio never knew if by this he meant to show that he feared nothing or, on the contrary, to excuse his sins. The old priest was tired. He stood up. He felt nauseated by everything he had heard, and wanted to be alone. But Rocco's voice rang out again.

"That's not all, Father."

"What else is there?" asked don Giorgio.

"I would like to make a gift to the Church."

"What kind of gift?"

"Everything, Father. Everything I own. All the riches accumulated over the years. Everything that makes me the richest man in Montepuccio today."

"I won't accept a thing from you. Your money is drenched with blood. How dare you even suggest such a thing, after everything you've just told me? Give it back to the people you stole it from, if remorse keeps you up at night."

"You know as well as I do that that's impossible. Most of the people I robbed are dead. And how could I ever find the others?"

"You need only distribute the money to the people of Montepuccio. To the poor. To the fishermen and their families."

"That's what I'd be doing by giving it to you. You are the Church, and the people of Montepuccio are your children. It's up to you to distribute it. If I did it myself, while still alive, I'd be giving these people tainted money and making them accomplices in crime. It's different if you do it. In your hands the money will be blessed."

What kind of man was this? Don Giorgio was dumbfounded by the way Rocco expressed himself. Such intelligence, such clarity for a brigand with no education. He began to imagine what Rocco Scorta might have been. A fine man, charismatic, with a glint in his eye that made one want to follow him to the ends of the earth.

"And what about your children?" asked the priest. "Will you add robbing your children to your list of crimes?"

Rocco smiled and answered softly.

"It's no gift to let them profit from ill-gotten gains. It would be encouraging them in sin."

The argument was good, too good. Don Giorgio had the feeling that it was all rhetoric. Rocco had smiled as he spoke; he didn't believe a word he was saying.

"What's the real reason?" asked the priest in a loud voice tinged with anger.

Rocco Scorta began to laugh. But he laughed too hard, and it made the priest turn pale. Rocco laughed like a demon.

"Don Giorgio," he said between peals of laughter, "let me die with a secret or two."

Father Zampanelli would think about this laughter for a long time to come. That laugh said it all. It bespoke a great desire for revenge that nothing could assuage. Rocco would have destroyed his family if he could have. Everything he owned must perish with him. His laughter was demented, like that of a man cutting off his fingers. It was the laughter of crime, turned against oneself.

"Do you realize what you are condemning them to?" asked the priest, who wanted to see this through to the end.

"Yes," Rocco answered coldly. "To life. Without rest."

Don Giorgio felt the weariness of the vanquished.

"So be it. I accept your gift. Everything you own. Your whole fortune. So be it. But don't imagine you're redeeming yourself by this."

"I don't, Father. I can't buy eternal rest. There could never be any for me. I want something else in return."

"What now?" asked the priest, who was at the end of his tether.

"I'm bequeathing the largest fortune Montepuccio has ever seen to the church. In exchange, I humbly ask that my family be buried like princes, in spite of the poverty that will be their lot from now on. Nothing more. After me, the Scortas will live in misery, since I am leaving them nothing. But their funerals must be as grand as possible. At the expense of the Church, to whom I am giving everything, so that she may honor her word. Let her bury us, one after the other, in proces-

sion. Make no mistake, don Giorgio. It's not out of pride
that I ask you this. It's for Montepuccio. I am going to
found a line of starvelings. They will be scorned. I know
the Montepuccians. They respect only money. Reduce
them to silence by burying the poorest among them
with the pomp accorded great lords. *The last shall be the
first.* Let this be true in Montepuccio at least. Generation
after generation. Let the Church remember her vow.
And may all of Montepuccio take their hats off when the
procession of the Mascalzones passes."

Rocco Scorta's eyes shone with a demented gleam
that made one think nobody could resist him. The old
priest went to look for a sheet of paper and wrote down
the terms of their agreement. When the ink had dried,
he handed the paper to Rocco, who signed it and said:
"Let it be thus."

he sun was already warming the façade of the church, its light flooding the countryside. Rocco Scorta and don Giorgio had spent the whole night talking. They parted without a word, without an embrace, as if they would see each other again that very evening.

Rocco went home. His family was already up. He didn't say a word. He ran his hand through his daughter's hair. Surprised by this unfamiliar gesture of affection, little Carmela looked at him wide-eyed and thoughtful. He then took to his bed and never got up again. He would not let them call a doctor. When the Mute, seeing the end draw near, wanted to go call the priest, he held her back by the arm and said, "Let don Giorgio sleep. He's had a hard night." The most he would accept was to let his wife send for two old women to help her keep watch over him. It was they who spread the news. "Rocco Scorta is on his deathbed. Rocco Scorta is dying." The townsfolk didn't believe it. Everyone remembered seeing him the day before, receptive, elegant, and strong. How could death have crept into his bones so fast?

The rumor now ran rampant. The townsfolk, their curiosity piqued, finally climbed the road to the property. They wanted to know the truth. A long column of rubberneckers crowded around the house. After a while, the boldest among them went inside. They were soon followed by everyone else. An inquisitive throng burst into the house, and it was unclear whether they were there to pay homage to the dying man or simply to confirm, to their relief, that he was indeed breathing his last.

When he saw the mob of townsfolk enter, Rocco sat up in bed. He gathered his remaining strength. His face was white, his body gaunt. He watched the crowd around him. There were sparks of rage in his eyes. Nobody dared make a move. Then the dying man began to speak:

"I am going down into my grave. The list of my crimes drags over my steps like a long mantle. I am Rocco Scorta Mascalzone, and I smile with pride. You expect remorse from me. You expect me to get down on my knees and pray for redemption. To beseech the Lord for clemency and beg pardon of those I have wronged. I spit on the ground. God's mercy is easy water for cowards to wash their faces in. I ask for nothing. I know what I've done, and I know what you're thinking. You go to your churches. You look at the frescoes of Hell that are painted there for your credulous minds. The little devils pulling in the tarnished souls by their feet, monsters with horns and cloven goat-feet gleefully tearing apart their tortured bodies. Spanking them, biting them, wringing them like dolls. The damned beg forgiveness. They get down on their knees and implore like women. But the demons with animal eyes know no pity. And you love it, because that is how it's supposed to be. You love it because you see justice in it. As I go down to my grave, you doom me to this unending medley of torments and cries. 'Rocco will soon suffer the punishment we see in the frescoes in our churches,' you tell yourselves. 'For all eternity.' But I am not trembling. I'm smiling the same smile that so often chilled you to the bone while I was alive. I am not afraid of your frescoes. Those little devils have never haunted my nights. I have sinned. I have killed and raped. Who ever stayed my hand? Who ever cast me down into nothingness to rid the earth of my presence? Nobody. The clouds continued to pass through the sky. On the days I stained my hands with blood, the weather was beautiful. Beautiful with a light that is like a pact between God and the world. What sort of pact can there be in the world I inhabit? None. The heavens are empty, and I can die smiling. I am a five-footed monster. I have a hyena's eyes and a killer's hands. I have made God withdraw everywhere I went. He has stepped aside to let me pass, just as you have done, in the streets of Montepuccio, holding your children tight. Today it is raining, and I leave the world without looking back. I have drunk. I have known pleasure. I have belched in the silence of churches. I have greedily devoured everything I could get my hands on. Today should be a day of celebration. The heavens should have opened, the angels' trumpets should have blasted in celebration of the news of my death. But there's nothing. It's raining. As if God were sad to see me go. Rubbish. I've lived a long time because the world is made in my image. It's all topsy turvy. I am a man. Rocco Scorta Mascalzone. I have no hope. I eat what I can. And you who despise me, you who condemn me to the most terrible torments, in the end you pronounced my name with admiration. The money I amassed has a lot to do with that. For though you spit on my crimes, you cannot help but feel in your hearts man's ancient, stinking respect for gold. Yes. And I've got a lot of it. More than any among you. I do. And I'm leaving nothing. I shall vanish with my knives, laughing like a thief. I've always done what I wanted, throughout my life. I am Rocco Scorta Mascalzone. Rejoice, I am dying."

When he'd finished saying his last words, he fell back in his bed. His strength had abandoned him. He died with his eyes open. Amidst the silence of the dumb-struck townsfolk. There was no death-rattle, no groaning. He died looking straight ahead.

he burial was arranged for the following day. That was when Montepuccio got its biggest surprise.

From the heights of the Scorta domain came the piercing music of a funeral procession, and moments later the townsfolk saw a long cortege of black-clad people enter the village, Father Zampanelli at its head, shaking a fine silver censer that filled the streets with a heavy, holy scent. The coffin was borne by six men. The town's patron saint, Sant'Elia, carried by six others, had been brought out for the occasion. The musicians played the saddest dirges of the land, slowly, in the cadenced tempo of a march. Never before had anyone been buried this way in Montepuccio. The procession went up the Corso, came to a stop in the central square, swept into the narrow streets of the old town, then circled back into the main square, stopped again, marched back down the Corso, and finally entered the church. Then, after a brief ceremony during which the priest announced that Rocco Scorta Mascalzone had bequeathed his entire fortune to the Church—triggering a buzz of astonishment and comment—the procession set off again to the poignant sounds of the brass section. The church bells punctuated the band's plaintive melodies. The whole village was there. And the same questions arose in everyone's mind: Was it really his entire fortune? How much was it worth? What would the priest do with it? What would become of the Mute? And the three children? They studied the poor woman's face, trying to guess if she'd been aware of her husband's last wishes, but could glean nothing from the widow's tired features. The whole village was there, and Rocco Scorta smiled in his grave. It had taken his entire life-time, but he had achieved what he'd wanted all along. To have Montepuccio under his thumb. To hold the whole town in the palm of his hand. By means of money, since money was the only way. And just when these clods thought they understood him, when they actually began to like him, to call him "don Rocco," when they had started paying homage to his fortune and kissing his hands, he'd thrown it all away in a great burst of laughter. That was what he'd wanted all along. Yes, Rocco smiled in his grave, no longer worrying about what he was leaving behind.

For the people of Montepuccio, it was clear. Rocco Scorta had transformed the curse that hung over his line. The Mascalzone were a race of bastards condemned to madness. Rocco had been the first, but the rest, no doubt, would have it worse. By giving away his fortune, Rocco Scorta was hoping to alter this curse. His family, hence-forth, would no longer be mad, but poor. And for all of Montepuccio, that seemed respectable. Rocco Scorta had not escaped. It was a high price to pay, but it was just. It gave his children a chance to be good Christians.

The three children huddled together before their father's grave. Raffaele was there too, holding Carmela's hand. They weren't crying. None of them felt real grief over the death of their father. It wasn't sorrow that made them clench their jaws; it was hatred. They understood that everything had been taken away from them, and that from now on the only thing they could count on was their own strength. They understood that a savage will had condemned them to poverty, and that this will was their father's. Domenico, Giuseppe, and Carmela stared at the hole in the ground at their feet and felt as if their whole lives were being buried. How would they get by tomorrow? With what money? And where, since even the farm had been given away? How strong would they have to be to fight the battles that awaited them? They remained huddled together, full of hatred for the days ahead. They understood. They already felt it in the way the others were looking at them: from now on, they were poor. So poor they could die.

love coming here. I've come here so many times. It's an old plot of land where only wild grasses grow, swept by the wind. You can still see a few lights in the town, just barely. And the tip of the church steeple, over there. There's nothing here. Just this old wooden bench, half-sunk into the ground. This is where I wanted to bring you, don Salvatore. This is where I'd like for us to sit. Do you know what this piece of furniture is? It's the old confessional from the church, the one that was used in the days of don Giorgio. Your predecessor replaced it. The movers took it out of the church and left it here. No one has touched it since. It has deteriorated. The paint is gone, the wood has aged. It has sunk into the earth. I often sit here. It's from my time.

I don't want to confess, don Salvatore, don't misunderstand me. If I've brought you here, if I've asked you to sit here beside me on this old wooden bench, it's not because I want your blessing. The Scortas never confess. My father was the last. Don't frown, I'm not insulting you. It's just that I am Rocco's daughter, and while I've hated him for a long time now, that doesn't change a thing. His blood flows in my veins.

I remember him on his deathbed. His body glistened with sweat. He was pale. Death was already coursing under his skin. He took a moment to look around him. The whole village was packed inside the tiny room. His eyes glanced over his wife, his children, and the crowd of people he had terrorized, and he said with a dying man's smile, "Rejoice, I am dying." Those words stung me as if I had been slapped in the face. "Rejoice, I am dying." The people of Montepuccio certainly did rejoice, but the three of us standing at his bedside stared at him blankly. What joy would this bring us? Why should we rejoice at his departure? His words were addressed to us all, without distinction. Rocco had always been alone against the rest of the world. I should have despised him. I should have hated him as only offended children can hate. But I couldn't, don Salvatore. I remembered a gesture he once made. Just before taking to his deathbed, he ran his hand through my hair, without a word. Something he never did. He passed his manly hand over my head, softly, and I never knew if this gesture was yet another curse or a sign of affection. I could never decide. I ended up thinking that it was both things at once. He caressed me the way a father caresses his daughter, and he left grief in my hair as an enemy would have done. By this gesture I became my father's daughter. He did not do it to my brothers. I am the only one to have been marked. All the weight has been on me. I am my father's only daughter. Domenico and Giuseppe were born quietly as the years went by. As if no parent had brought them into the world. For me, there was that gesture. He chose me. I am proud of this, and that he might have done it to damn me doesn't change a thing. Can you understand this?

I am Rocco's daughter, don Salvatore. Don't expect me to confess. The pact between the church and the Scortas has been broken. I brought you to this open-air confessional because I didn't want to meet you in church. I didn't want to speak to you with my head bowed, my voice trembling like a penitent's. This sort of place is appropriate for the Scortas. The wind is blowing and night surrounds us. No one can hear us, only the stones that echo our voices. The years haven't been kind to the wood we are sitting on. These shiny boards have heard so many confessions, they've been burnished by the sorrows of the world. Thousands of timid voices have whispered their crimes here, admitted their sins, revealed their ugliness. This is where don Giorgio listened to them. This is where he listened to my father until he felt sick to his stomach, the evening he confessed. So many words, don Salvatore, have seeped into these boards. On windy evenings like this, I can hear them resurfacing. Thousands of guilty whispers, accumulated over the years. Stifled sobs, shameful confessions. They all come out, like great mists of sorrow with which the wind scents the hills. That helps me. This is the only place I can speak. On this old bench. Only here. But I'm not confessing. I don't expect any blessings from you. I'm not asking to be washed clean of my sins. They are there, inside me. I shall carry them to my grave. But I want things to be said. And then I will disappear. Leaving maybe a scent behind, in the wind on summer evenings. The scent of a life that will blend with the smell of the rocks and wild grasses.

III

THE PAUPERS' RETURN

"Wait!" cried Giuseppe, "wait!"

Domenico and Carmela stopped, turned round, and beheld their brother hopping on one foot a few yards behind them.

"What's wrong?" asked Domenico.

"I've got a pebble in my shoe."

He sat down at the side of the road and began untying his shoelaces.

"It's been torturing me for at least two hours," he added.

"Two hours?" asked Domenico.

"Yes," confirmed Giuseppe.

"And you can't put up with it a little longer? We're almost there."

"Do you want me to be limping when I make my re-entry into town?"

In a peremptory tone, Domenico let fly a resounding "*Ma vaffanculo!*"* Their sister burst out laughing.

They took a break at the side of the road. Deep down they were happy to have a chance to catch their breath and contemplate the distance still left to travel. They blessed the little pebble tormenting Giuseppe; it was the excuse they'd been waiting for. Giuseppe removed his shoe slowly, to savor the moment. Montepuccio now lay at their feet. They gazed down at their native village with a kind of hunger in their eyes, and the apprehension that emigrants feel at the moment of their return—the old, irrepressible fear that during their absence, everything had disappeared. That the streets would no longer look the same, and the people they'd known were gone or, worse yet, would greet them with frowns of disgust and sidelong glances, as if to say, "Oh, you again?" There by the side of the road, they all shared this fear, and the pebble in Giuseppe's shoe was the tool of Providence. They wanted time to take in the town at a glance, catch their breath, and make the sign of the Cross before beginning their descent.

Scarcely a year had passed since their departure, but they had aged. Their faces had hardened. Their eyes had acquired a harsh strength. A whole life had gone by: a life of anguish, scrapping, and unexpected joy.

Domenico—whom everyone called "*Mimì vaffan-culo*" because every statement that came out of his mouth ended with that injunction, which he uttered in a drawling manner as though it was not an insult but a new form of punctuation—Domenico had become a man. He looked ten years older than his age. He had a thick, unhandsome face and a piercing gaze that seemed made for gauging the worth of the person he was talking to. He was strong, with broad hands, but all his energy went into sizing up, as quickly as possible, the person in front of him. "Can I trust this man?" "Is there any money to be made here?" Such questions no longer formed in his mind; they had, as it were, entered his blood.

Giuseppe, for his part, had retained his childish features. Two years Domenico's junior, he still had a round, chubby face despite the months that had passed. Within their little group, he instinctively concentrated his whole being on defusing conflicts. He was often cheerful and had so much confidence in his brother and sister that he rarely lost hope in tomorrow. His nickname was "*Peppe pancia piena*,"* because having a full belly was the state he loved most in life. To eat his fill, and beyond, was his obsession. A day was considered good when one had eaten a meal worthy of the name. And if there were two decent meals, the day was exceptional and put Giuseppe in a good mood that might last several days. How many times, on the road that took them from Naples to Montepuccio, had he smiled when remembering a plate of gnocchi or pasta he'd devoured the previous day? He would start talking to himself, in the dust of the journey, smiling blissfully, as though he no longer felt tired but had found some inner, joyous strength that would make him suddenly cry out: "*Madonna, che pasta!…*"* And eagerly ask his brother, "Remember, Mimì?" Then came the endless description of the pasta in question—the texture, the flavor, the sauce—and he would persist, "Do you remember that *sugo*,* Mimì, how red it was? You could taste the meat that had simmered in it. Remember?" And Mimì, exasperated by the raving of his lunatic brother, would inevitably let fly, "*Ma vaffanculo*, you and your pasta!" This meant there was still a long road ahead, his legs hurt, and in fact there was no telling exactly when they might eat such good pasta again.

Carmela, whom her brothers affectionately called
Miuccia, was still a child, and still had a child's body and
voice. But these last few months had transformed her
more than her brothers. She had been the source of the
greatest misfortunes and the greatest joys their little
group had known during their travels. No one ever
reproached her for it, but she did understand one thing:
It had all been her fault. Yet it was also thanks to her that
all had been saved *in extremis*, and this had kindled in
her a sense of responsibility and intelligence well
beyond her years. In everyday life she remained a little
girl, laughing at her brothers' jokes, but when fate
turned against them, she gave out orders and gritted her
teeth. It was she who, on the road back home, held the
donkey's reins. Her two brothers had put everything
they owned—the donkey and the jumble of sundry
objects it was carrying—in her hands. There were suitcases, a teapot, some Dutch porcelain dishes, a wicker
chair, an entire set of copper pots and pans, and blankets. The donkey bore its burden conscientiously. None
of these objects, taken by itself, was worth very much,
but all together they constituted the accumulation of a
lifetime. Carmela also carried the purse in which they'd
put the savings amassed during their journey. She
watched over this treasure with the avidity of the poor.

"Do you think they've lit the paper lanterns?"
Giuseppe's voice had broken the silence of the hills.
Three days earlier, a horseman had passed them. After a
bit of discussion, the Scortas explained that they were

going back home to Montepuccio. The horseman had promised he would announce their return, and Giuseppe wondered if they would be welcomed by the lighting of paper lanterns on the Corso Garibaldi, the way it was done in the past when emigrants came back. To celebrate the return of the "Americans."

"Of course not," said Domenico. "Paper lanterns…," he added with a shrug, and silence enveloped them anew.

Of course not. They could never expect paper lanterns for the Scortas. Giuseppe looked sad for a moment. Domenico had spoken in a tone that seemed to allow no challenge, yet he too had wondered the same thing. Now he thought about it again. Yes, paper lanterns, just for them. The whole town would be there. Even little Carmela thought about it. Stepping onto the Corso Garibaldi and recognizing the teary, smiling faces. All three of them were dreaming of this. Why not, after all? Paper lanterns. It would be wonderful.

The wind had picked up, sweeping away the scent of the hills. The last glow of daylight faded softly. Then, without a word, in a single movement, they set out again, drawn towards the village as if by a magnet, at once impatient and fearful.

They entered Montepuccio at night. Corso Garibaldi lay there before them, just as they had left it ten months before. But it was empty. The wind swept down the thoroughfare and whistled over the heads of cats that high-tailed away with backs arched. There wasn't a living soul about. The village was asleep, and the donkey's hooves resonated in the street with the very sound of solitude.

Domenico, Giuseppe, and Carmela walked on, teeth clenched. They didn't have the heart to look at one another. They didn't have the heart to speak. They were angry at themselves for falling prey to that stupid hope— paper lanterns… What goddamned paper lanterns?— and now they clenched their fists in silence.

They passed in front of what was still, at the time of their departure, Luigi Zacalonia's haberdashery. Clearly something had happened; the sign was on the ground, the windows shattered. Nothing was sold or bought there anymore. This upset them. Not that they'd been faithful customers, but any change at all in Montepuccio seemed like a bad omen. They wanted everything to be the way they'd left it, for time not to have damaged anything during their absence. If Luigi Zacalonia no longer had his haberdashery, God only knew what other disappointments they should expect.

When they'd gone a little further down the Corso, they noticed the silhouette of a man curled up against a wall and sleeping right there, in the wind. They thought at first that he must be a drunkard, but when they were only a few steps away, Giuseppe started shouting, "Raffaele! It's Raffaele!" This made the boy give a start. He leapt to his feet. The Scortas were yelling with joy. Raffaele's eyes glistened with happiness, but he was also cursing himself. He felt mortified for having so foolishly missed the moment of his friends' arrival. He had prepared himself for it, vowing to stay up all night if necessary; but finally, little by little, his strength had abandoned him and he had drifted off to sleep.

"You're here," he said with tears in his eyes. "Mimì, Peppe, you're here. My friends, let me look at you! Miuccia! And to think I was asleep. What a jerk! I wanted to see you arrive from far away."

They kissed, embraced, patted one another on the back. One thing, at least, had not changed in Montepuccio. Raffaele was still here. But the young man didn't know which way to turn. He hadn't even noticed the donkey and the mass of objects it was carrying. He'd been immediately struck by Carmela's beauty, but this only added to his confusion and stammering.

Raffaele finally managed to articulate a few words. He begged his friends to come and stay with him. It was late. The village was asleep. The Scortas' reunion with Montepuccio could certainly wait till tomorrow.

The Scortas accepted his invitation and had to fight to prevent their friend from carrying all their bags and suitcases on his back. He now lived in a small, low house near the port. A miserable house, cut out of the rock and whitewashed. Raffaele had prepared a surprise for his friends. The moment he'd learned of the Scortas' imminent arrival, he'd set to work at once and hadn't stopped. He'd bought some big round loaves of white bread, put a meat sauce on the stove to simmer, and prepared some pasta. He wanted to have a feast to welcome his friends home.

When they were all settled in around the small wooden table and Raffaele brought out a great platter of hand-made *orecchiette* swimming in a thick tomato sauce, Giuseppe started crying. He'd been reunited with the flavors of his native village. Reunited with his old friend. He didn't need anything else. All the paper lanterns in Corso Garibaldi could not have satisfied him any more than the dish of steaming *orecchiette* he was about to devour.

They ate. They crunched the big slices of toasted white bread that Raffaele had rubbed with tomatoes, olive oil, and salt. They let the pasta, dripping with sauce, melt in their mouths. They ate without realizing that Raffaele was watching them with a sad look on his face. After a little while, Carmela noticed their friend's silence.

"What's wrong, Raffaele?" she asked.

The young man smiled. He didn't want to speak before his friends had finished eating. What he had to say could easily wait a few more minutes. He wanted to see them finish their meal. For Giuseppe to savor it in full and have the time and leisure to lick his plate to his satisfaction.

"Raffaele?" Carmela persisted.

"So, tell me. New York, what was it like?"

He'd thrown out the question with a feigned enthusiasm. Carmela wasn't fooled.

"You first, Raffaele. Tell us what you have to say."

The two brothers looked up from their plates. Their sister's tone had alerted them that some surprise was in the air. Everyone stared at Raffaele. His face was pale.

"What I have to say…" he muttered, unable to finish his sentence. The Scortas froze. "Your mother…the Mute…" he continued, "well, two months ago she passed away."

He hung his head. The Scortas said nothing. They were waiting. Raffaele realized he should say more. He had to tell them everything. So he looked back up, and his grief-stricken voice filled the room with sadness.

The Mute had been suffering from malaria. During the first weeks following her children's departure, she had managed to cope, but then her strength began to decline rapidly. She tried to buy time, hoping to hold on until her family returned or at least until she had some news of them. But she didn't make it, succumbing to a violent episode.

"Did don Giorgio bury her with dignity?" asked Domenico.

His question remained a long time unanswered. Raffaele was in agony. What he had to say was wrenching his guts. But he had to drink the cup down to the dregs and leave nothing out.

"Don Giorgio died long before she did. He died like an old man, with a smile on his lips and his hands folded on his chest."

"How was our mother buried?" asked Carmela, who felt that Raffaele had not answered the question, and that his silence masked a further torment.

"I couldn't do anything about it," Raffaele muttered. "I got there too late. I was out at sea for two whole days. By the time I got back, she was already buried. It was the new priest who took care of it. They buried her in the common grave. I couldn't do anything about it."

The Scortas' faces now hardened with rage. Jaws clenched tight, eyes dark. Those words, "common grave," echoed in their heads like a slap.

"What's the new priest's name?" asked Domenico.

"Don Carlo Bozzoni," replied Raffaele.

"We'll go see him tomorrow," asserted Domenico, and they all gathered from his voice that he already knew what he would demand, but that he didn't want to talk about it tonight.

They went to bed without finishing the meal. Nobody could say anything more. It was best to remain silent and let the sorrow of mourning sweep over them.

*T*he following day, Carmela, Giuseppe, Domenico and Raffaele got up for matins. They met the new village priest in the cold morning air.

"Father," Domenico cried out.

"Yes, my children, what can I do for you?" he replied in a honied voice.

"We're the children of the Mute."

"Whose children?"

"The Mute's."

"That's not a name," said don Carlo, with a smile on his lips.

"That was hers," Carmela cut in, dryly.

"Tell me what her Christian name was," the priest resumed.

"She had no other name."

"What can I do for you?"

"She died a few months ago," said Domenico. "You buried her in the common grave."

"I remember. Yes. My most heartfelt condolences, my children. But don't be sad. Your mother is now at the side of Our Lord."

"We've come to see you about the burial," Carmela cut in again.

"You said it yourselves. She was buried with dignity."

"She's a Scorta."

"Yes, a Scorta. So be it. Fine. You see, she did have a name after all."

"She must be buried like a Scorta," Carmela resumed.

"We buried her like a Christian," don Bozzoni corrected her.

Domenico was white with rage. He said sharply:

"No, Father. Like a Scorta. It's written here."

He handed don Bozzoni the paper on which Rocco and don Giorgio had signed their pact. The priest read in silence. Anger rose to his cheeks and he burst out:

"What's this nonsense supposed to mean? This is unbelievable! It's superstition, that's what it is. Magic, I don't know what. By what authority did this don Giorgio sign in the Church's name? It's heresy. A Scorta! Imagine that. And you call yourselves Christians. Pagans full of secret ceremonies, that's what the people here are. A Scorta! She was cast into the earth like everyone else. That was all she could expect."

"Father," Giuseppe tried, "the Church made a pact with our family."

But the priest would not let him speak. He was already shouting:

"This is madness! A pact with the Scortas. You are out of your mind."

With an abrupt gesture, he pushed his way to the church's entrance and disappeared inside.

*T*he Scortas' absence had prevented them from per-
forming a sacred duty: digging their mother's grave
themselves. Filial piety demands this final gesture of
sons. Now that they were back, they were determined to
honor their mother's mortal remains. The loneliness, the
common grave, the flouted pact: these were too many
affronts to bear. They decided that they would arm
themselves with shovels and go dig up the Mute that very
night. So that she could rest in a pit all her own, dug by
her own sons. Too bad if it was outside the wall of the
cemetery. Better that than the nameless earth of a
common grave for eternity.

At nightfall, they met as agreed. Raffaele brought
the shovels. It was cold. Like thieves they slipped inside
the cemetery walls.

"Mimì?" asked Giuseppe.

"What is it?"

"Are you sure we're not committing a crime?"

Before Domenico could even answer his brother,
Carmela's voice rang out:

"It's this common grave that's a sacrilege."

Giuseppe then grabbed his shovel with determination and concluded:

"You're right, Miuccia. Let's get going."

They dug into the cold earth of the common grave without a word. The farther they dug, the harder it was to lift each new shovelful. They felt as if they risked waking the great mass of the dead at any moment. They tried not to tremble. Not to stagger in the face of the nauseating stench rising up from the earth.

At last their shovels struck the wood of a coffin. It took great strength and perseverance to extract it. On the pine lid, the name "Scorta" had been carved with a knife. This was where their mother lay. Inside this ugly box. Buried like a pauper. No marble, no ceremony. They hoisted her up onto their shoulders like thieves and headed out of the cemetery. They walked a bit along the enclosure wall until they reached a small embankment where they could no longer be seen by anyone. Here they set her down. Now they needed only to dig a hole. So that the Mute could feel the breath of her sons in the night. When they were about to begin, Giuseppe turned to Raffaele and asked:

"You going to dig with us?"

Raffaele looked stunned. It wasn't only help that Giuseppe was asking of him; it wasn't only to share the toil and sweat. No, what he was asking of him was to bury the Mute exactly as if he'd been one of her own sons. Raffaele was white as a sheet. Giuseppe and Domenico looked at him, awaiting his answer. Clearly Giuseppe had asked him on behalf of all three Scortas. Nobody had shown any surprise. They waited for Raffaele to decide. In front of the Mute's grave, Raffaele grabbed a shovel, tears in his eyes. "Of course," he said.

It was like becoming, in turn, a Scorta himself. As if the corpse of the poor woman were giving him her maternal blessing. From now on he would be their brother. As if the same blood flowed in their veins. Their brother. He clutched the shovel tight to keep from sobbing. The moment he began shoveling, he raised his head and his eyes fell upon Carmela. There she was beside them, still and silent, watching them work. He felt a twinge in his heart. A sense of deep regret welled up in his eyes. Miuccia. How beautiful she was. From now on he would have to look at her with a brother's eyes. He smothered this regret in the deepest part of himself, put his head down, and turned the earth with all his might.

When they had completed their task and the coffin was again covered with earth, they sat for a while in silence. They didn't want to leave without a last moment to collect themselves. A long time went by, then Domenico spoke. "We have no relations. We are the Scortas, all four of us. That's what we've decided. That name will have to keep us warm from now on. Begging the Mute's pardon, today is the real day of our birth."

It was cold. They kept their heads down a long time, looking at the turned earth, huddling close together. And indeed, that name, Scorta, was enough to keep them warm. Raffaele was weeping quietly. He'd been given a family, two brothers and a sister, for whom he was ready to give his life. Yes, from this moment on, he would be the fourth Scorta. He swore it over the freshly turned earth of the Mute's grave. He would carry their name. Raffaele Scorta. And the scorn of the Montepuccians would only make him laugh. He would fight, body and soul, alongside those he loved, those he thought he had lost when they went to America and left him as alone as a madman. Raffaele Scorta. Yes. He vowed he would be equal to his new name.

I've come to tell you about the trip to New York, don Salvatore. If it wasn't night, I wouldn't dare speak. But there is darkness all around, you are quietly smoking, and I must have my say.

After my father's funeral, don Giorgio called us together and told us his plan. He had found a small house in the old town, where our mother, the Mute, could live. It would be poor, but dignified. She could move in as soon as possible. For us, on the other hand, another solution had to be found. Life here in Montepuccio had nothing to offer us. We would drag our poverty around the village streets with the rage of people whom destiny had stripped of their rank. Nothing good could come of this. Don Giorgio did not want to condemn us to a life of misery and squalor. He had a better idea. He would arrange to get three tickets aboard a ship going from Naples to New York. The church would pay. We would leave for the land where the poor build buildings as tall as the sky, and fortune sometimes lines the pockets of the downtrodden.

We said yes right away. That same night, I remember, crazy visions of imaginary cities filled my head, and I repeated over and over, like a prayer, the name that made my eyes glisten: New York. . . New York. . .

When we left Montepuccio for Naples—accompanied by don Giorgio, who had wanted to escort us all the way to

*the pier—the earth seemed to groan under our feet, as
though cursing these children who had the audacity to try
to abandon her. We left the Gargano, went down into the
vast, dreary plain of Foggia, and crossed the entire Italian
peninsula before reaching Naples. That labyrinth of
shouts, squalor, and heat left us wide-eyed. The big city
smelled of herring and rotting fish. The streets of Spac-
canapoli* swarmed with children with bloated bellies and
toothless mouths.*

*Don Giorgio brought us to the port, and we boarded
one of those ocean liners built to carry starvelings from one
point of the globe to another amidst great sighs of petro-
leum. We took our places among people like us. The poor
of Europe, with hunger in their eyes. Whole families and
solitary urchins. Like everyone else, we held each other by
the hand so as not to get lost in the crowd. Like everyone
else, we couldn't sleep the first night, fearing that treach-
erous hands might steal the blanket we shared. Like
everyone else, we wept once the huge ship left the bay of
Naples. "Life is beginning," Domenico said in a low voice.
Italy disappeared before our eyes. Like everyone else, we
turned towards America, awaiting the day when her coastline would come into view, hoping, in strange dreams, that
everything would be different there, the colors, the smells,
the laws, the people. Everything. Bigger. Gentler. During
the crossing, we spent hours on the deck, clinging to the
railing, trying to conjure up this continent where even
wretched folk like us were welcome. The days were long,
but that didn't matter, since the dreams we dreamt needed*

hours and hours to take shape in our minds. The days were long, but we let them flow by happily, since the world was beginning.

At last we arrived at the port of New York. The ship headed slowly towards tiny Ellis Island. I shall never forget the joy of that day, don Salvatore. We danced and we cried. A wild excitement had taken hold on the deck. Everyone wanted to see the new world. We cheered every fishing trawler we passed. Everyone pointed at the buildings of Manhattan. Our eyes devoured every detail of the coastline.

When the ship finally docked, we went ashore amidst a clamor of impatience and joy. The crowd filled the great hall of the little island. We heard languages spoken which at first we took for Milanese or Roman dialect, until we had to acknowledge that what was happening here was much vaster. The whole world surrounded us. We could have felt lost. We were foreigners. We understood nothing. But we were filled with a strange feeling, don Salvatore. We were sure that we were where we belonged. Amidst all those lost souls, in that confusion of voices and accents, we felt at home. The people around us were our brothers and sisters. By the filth they wore on their faces, and the fear that twisted their guts. Don Giorgio had been right. This was where we belonged, in this country that was like no other. We were in America, and we weren't afraid anymore. Our life in Montepuccio seemed far away and ugly. We were in America, and our nights were filled with joyous, hungry dreams.

Don Salvatore, pay no attention if my voice cracks and I lower my eyes; I am going to tell you something that nobody else knows. Nobody but the Scortas. Listen. The night is long and I'm going to tell you everything.

Upon arrival we went ashore, excited to be leaving the ship. We were happy and impatient. We had to take our places and wait, but this didn't matter to us. We waited in endless lines. We participated in strange procedures that we didn't understand. Everything was slow. We were directed to one counter, then another. We kept very close together so as not to get lost. Hours passed and the crowd seemed to get smaller. People grew restless. Domenico kept moving forward, leading us on. At one point, he announced that we were going to be examined by some doctors, and that we had to stick out our tongues, take a couple of deep breaths, and not to be shy about opening our shirts if we were asked. We had to submit to everything, but it didn't matter; we were ready to wait for days if necessary. The country was right there, within reach.

When I went before the doctor, he gestured for me to stop. He looked into my eyes and, without saying a word, made a mark on my hand in chalk. I wanted to ask why, but I was signaled to proceed to another room. A second doctor listened to my chest a long time. He asked me some questions, but I didn't understand him and didn't know what to answer. I was a young girl, don Salvatore, a young girl whose knees quaked before these strangers leaning over me as if I were some farm animal. A little later, my brothers joined me. They'd had to fight to get through.

After an interpreter arrived, we understood what was the matter. I had an infection. I had, in fact, been sick on the boat for several days. Fever, diarrhea, red eyes, but I thought it would pass. I was a young girl on my way to New York, and I didn't think any illness could stop me. The man spoke for a long time, but all I understood was that, for me, the journey was over. The ground gave way beneath my feet. I'd been rejected, don Salvatore. It was all over. I was ashamed and hung my head to avoid my brothers' eyes. They stood silently beside me. I stared at the long line of immigrants who continued to pass in front of us, and I could only think of one thing: "They let all those people in, even that sickly one over there, and even that old guy who might drop dead in two months' time. They let them all in. Why not me?"

Then the interpreter spoke again. "You'll have to go back home. Don't worry, there's no charge for the journey. The boat is free. Free." That's all he could say, just that one word. That's when Giuseppe suggested to Domenico that he continue on alone. "Mimì, you go on. I'll stay with Miuccia."

I didn't say a thing. Our lives were in the balance, for years to come, in this discussion between two rooms. But I didn't say a thing. I couldn't. I hadn't the strength. I was ashamed. Simply ashamed. I could only listen and put my fate in my brothers' hands. Our three lives were at stake here, and it was all my fault. Everything depended on their decision. Giuseppe repeated, "It's better this way, Mimì. You go on, you go on alone. Me, I'll stay with Miuccia. We'll go home. We'll try again later."

Time stood still. Believe me, don Salvatore, I aged sev-

eral years during that one minute. Everything was sus-
pended. I was waiting. Waiting for destiny to weigh our
three lives and choose the fate it saw fit. Then Domenico
spoke: "No. We came together and we'll leave together."
Giuseppe wanted to insist, but Domenico cut him off. He'd
made up his mind. He gritted his teeth and made a
brusque gesture with his hand that I'll never forget: "It's all
three of us or nothing. They don't want us. They can go
fuck themselves."

IV

THE SILENT ONES' TOBACCO SHOP

The disinterment of the Mute's body and her second burial sent a tremor through Montepuccio. There was now a mound of freshly turned earth outside the cemetery that couldn't be ignored. It was an unacceptable wart on the face of the village. The people of Montepuccio were afraid that word would spread. That everyone in the region would know and point the finger at them. They were afraid that people would say that in Montepuccio they did not bury their dead properly, that in their cemeteries they turned the earth as in a field. This wild grave, apart from the rest, was like a permanent reproach. Don Carlo was still fuming. He went about casting aspersions. He spoke of grave-robbers. For him, the Scortas had crossed the line. To dig up the earth and extract a body from its final resting place was the work of heathens. He would never have imagined that such barbarians could exist in Italy.

One night, unable to stand it any longer, he went so far as to pull up the wooden crucifix that the Scortas had planted in the mound of earth and broke it in a fit of rage. The grave remained in that state for a few days. Then the cross reappeared. The priest prepared a second punitive expedition, but every time he tore away the cross it reappeared. Don Carlo thought he was fighting

the Scortas, but he was wrong. He was engaged in a con-
test of wills against the whole town. Every day, anonymous
hands, repelled by that miserable, unmarked grave, would
plant another wooden cross. After a few weeks of this
game, a delegation of townsfolk went to don Carlo to persuade him to change his mind. They asked him to hold a
ceremony and allow the Mute to be reintegrated into the
cemetery. They even suggested that, to avoid having to dig
up the poor woman a second time, the cemetery wall be
broken and rebuilt in such a way as to include the excom-
municated woman. Don Carlo would hear none of it. The
scorn he felt for the villagers only increased. He became
sullen and prone to violent outbursts.

From that moment on, all of Montepuccio began to
hate Father Bozzoni. One after another, the villagers
swore they wouldn't set foot in the church so long as
that "idiot priest from the North" presided there. In fact,
what the Scortas had demanded of him was something
the whole town had expected from the start. When
they'd first heard of the Mute's death, they immediately
thought that the funeral would be as grand as Rocco's.
Don Carlo's decision had revolted them. Who did this
priest, who wasn't even from these parts, think he was to
come here and change the unalterable rules of the village? The decision of the "new guy," as the women at the
market called don Carlo, was seen as an insult to the
memory of the beloved don Giorgio. And this was
unforgivable. The "new guy" had no respect for tradition. He came from who-knows-where to impose his

own law. The Scortas had been insulted. By extension, the whole town felt insulted. No one had ever witnessed such a burial before. This man, though a priest, had no respect for anything, and Montepuccio wanted no part of him. But there was another reason for this savage reprobation. Fear. The old terror of Rocco Scorta Mascalzone, never wholly forgotten. By thus burying the woman who had been his wife, don Carlo was condemning the village to Rocco's wrath. They remembered the crimes he had committed during his lifetime, and trembled at the thought of what he might be capable of in death. There was no doubt about it, an evil fate awaited Montepuccio. An earthquake. Or a bad drought. Rocco Scorta Mascalzone's breath was already in the air. You could feel it in the hot evening wind.

The people of Montepuccio viewed the Scortas with an inextricable mixture of scorn, pride, and fear. In normal times, the village ignored Carmela, Domenico, and Giuseppe. They were merely three hungry souls, a brigand's spawn. But the moment anyone wanted to touch a single hair on their heads or insult the memory of Rocco the Savage, a kind of maternal instinct awoke in the whole village, and it defended them like a she-wolf defending her young. "The Scortas are good-for-nothings, but they belong to us"—such was how most of the people in Montepuccio saw things. And, after all, the Scortas had gone to New York. This conferred something sacred on them, making them untouchable in the eyes of most of the townsfolk.

In the space of a few days, the church was deserted. No one went to Mass anymore. No one greeted don Carlo in the streets. He had been given a new nickname, which signed his death warrant: "the Milanese." Montepuccio sank into an ancestral paganism. People practiced all sorts of ceremonies in the shadow of the church. In the hills they danced the tarantella. The fishermen worshiped fish-headed idols, hybrids of patron saints and water spirits. In winter, old women spoke with the dead in the recesses of their homes. On several occasions, people practiced exorcisms on simpletons believed to be possessed by the devil. Dead animals were found outside the doors of certain houses. Revolt was brewing.

A few months passed until the day when Montepuccio, late one morning, was gripped by an unwonted agitation. A rumor was circulating that made people's jaws drop. They lowered their voices when they spoke of it. Old women crossed themselves. Something had happened that morning, and everyone was talking about it. Father Bozzoni was dead. And that wasn't the worst of it. He had died in strange circumstances that common decency prevented one from describing. For many hours, nothing more was known. Then, as the day progressed and the sun warmed the fronts of the houses, more details began to emerge. Don Carlo had been found in the hills, a day's walk from Montepuccio, naked as a worm, tongue hanging out like a slaughtered calf. How was this possible? What was don Carlo doing all alone in the hills so far from his parish? From one gathering to another, over Sunday coffee, the men and women of Montepuccio asked themselves these same questions. But there was more astounding news yet to come. Around eleven o'clock, people learned that don Carlo's body had been scorched all over by the sun—even his face, though the corpse had been found face down. It was obvious; he had been naked before he died. And he had been walking about naked, under the sun, for hours on end, until his skin had blistered and his feet bled and he died of exhaustion and dehydration. The central mystery remained: Why had he set off like that, alone, into the hills, at the hottest time of day? This question would fuel many a conversation in Montepuccio for years to come. But on that day, in order to arrive at a consensus, at least temporarily, it was agreed that, to all appearances, his solitude had driven him insane. He must have woken up one morning in the grips of madness and decided to leave the village he so despised, by whatever means possible. The sun had got the better of him. That grotesque death, that nakedness—so obscene for a man of the Church—confirmed the villagers in their conviction. Clearly, this don Carlo was a worthless fool.

Raffaele blanched when he heard the news. He had them repeat it to him, and stood as if rooted to the square, where speculations swirled about like wind in the streets. He had to know more, to hear all the details, to confirm that it was all true. He seemed afflicted by the news, which surprised those who knew him. He was a Scorta. He should have rejoiced at this passing. Raffaele lingered a long time, unable to tear himself away from the outdoor café. Then, when he had to face the facts, when there was no more doubt in his mind that the priest was dead, he spat on ground and muttered, "That rascal found a way to take me with him."

The previous day, the two men had crossed paths on one of the trails through the hills. Raffaele was coming up from the sea, and don Carlo was taking a solitary walk. Trudging along the paths in the countryside had become the priest's only distraction. At first, the quarantine in which the townsfolk had placed him had enraged him; then, as the weeks went by, it plunged him deep into a hopeless solitude. His mind wandered. He lost his bearings amidst such isolation. Staying in the village became a heavy cross to bear. He found no respite except in these long walks.

Raffaele was the first to speak. He thought perhaps he could use this opportunity to attempt a last negotiation.

"Don Carlo," he said, "you have offended us. It's time to go back on your decision."

"You are a bunch of degenerates," the priest shouted by way of an answer. "The Lord sees you, and He will punish you."

Anger rose up in Raffaele, but he tried to restrain himself and continued:

"You hate us. So be it. But the one you're punishing has nothing to do with this. The Mute has a right to be buried in the cemetery."

"She was in the cemetery before you dug her up. She

got what she deserved, sinner that she was, for having spawned such a band of heathens."

Raffaele turned pale. It seemed to him as if the hills themselves commanded him to answer this insult.

"You're unworthy of the frock you are wearing, Bozzoni. Do you hear me? You're a rat hiding behind a cassock. Give back that cassock, or I'll kill you."

And he leapt at the priest like a snarling dog. He grabbed him by the neck and with one furious swipe of the hand ripped off his collar. The priest was beside himself, choking with helplessness. Raffaele wouldn't release his grip. He yelled like a madman, "Strip, you son of a bitch, strip!" shredding the priest's cassock with all his might and pummeling him all the while.

He didn't calm down until he had undressed Father Bozzoni completely. Don Carlo surrendered. He cried like a baby, covering his torso with his plump hands. He muttered prayers, as if he were up against a horde of heretics. Raffaele rejoiced with all the ferocity of vengeance, "That's how you'll go around from now on: naked as a worm. You have no right to wear this habit. If I find you wearing it again, I'll kill you, understand?"

Don Carlo did not answer. He walked away, weeping, and disappeared. He never came back. This episode had sent him over the edge once and for all. He wandered through the hills like a lost child, paying no mind to fatigue or the sun. He wandered about for a long time before collapsing, exhausted, on the southern ground he so detested.

Raffaele remained a while at the spot where he had thrashed the priest. He couldn't move. He was waiting for his anger to die down, trying to get a grip on himself so he could return to the village without having his expression betray him. The priest's torn cassock lay at his feet. He couldn't take his eyes off of it. A ray of sunshine made him blink. Something glinted in the light. He bent over without thinking and picked up a gold watch. Had he left at that moment, he probably would have thrown it away in disgust a bit further on, but he didn't move. He felt that he hadn't seen things through. Slowly, warily, he bent down again, gathered up the torn cassock and went through the pockets. He emptied don Bozzoni's wallet and left it a little further up the path, open, like a deboned carcass. He squeezed the wad of bills and the gold watch in his fist, an ugly, demented grin on his face.

That rascal found a way to take me with him."

Raffaele had just realized that their altercation had led to a man's death, and even though he kept repeating that he hadn't killed anyone, he knew full well that this death would forever weigh on his conscience. He could still see the priest, naked, crying like a child, going off into the hills like a poor soul condemned to exile. "So I'm damned," he said to himself, "damned by that jerk, who wasn't worth the spit on my tongue."

Around midday, Father Bozzoni's body was brought back to Montepuccio on the back of a donkey. The corpse had been covered with a sheet, not so much to keep the flies off as to make sure the priest's nudity didn't shock the women and children.

Once it arrived in Montepuccio, something unexpected happened. The donkey's owner, a taciturn peasant, deposited the body in front of the church and declared loud and clear that he had done his duty and had to go back to his field. The body remained there, wrapped in a sheet, covered in dirt. People looked at it. Nobody moved. The Montepuccians bore grudges. Nobody wanted to bury it. Nobody wanted to participate in the ceremony or carry the coffin. Besides, who would say Mass? The priest from San Giocondo was away in Bari.

By the time he got back, don Carlo's body would be decomposing. At a certain point the sun's heat became overwhelming, and they ended up agreeing that if they left the Milanese's body out there, it wouldn't be long before it stank like carrion. That would be too sweet a revenge for the priest. To befoul Montepuccio. Spread sickness, why not? No, it was better to bury him. Not out of any sense of decency or charity, but to make sure he did no more harm. They decided to dig a hole behind the cemetery, on the other side of the wall. Four men were chosen by lots. They threw him into the ground, without any sacrament. In silence. Don Carlo was buried like a heathen, without a prayer to soften the bite of the sun.

This death was a big event for the people of Montepuccio, but the rest of the world hardly gave it a thought. After don Carlo's death, the village was once again forgotten by the episcopate. That suited them just fine. They were used to it. Sometimes, when passing the closed church, they even muttered amongst themselves, "Better nobody than a new Bozzoni," fearing that the Church, in a kind of divine punishment, might appoint them another man from the North who would treat them like dirt, mock their customs, and refuse to baptize their children.

The heavens seemed to have heard them. Nobody came and the church remained shut, like the palaces of those great families that disappear all at once, leaving behind them a scent of grandeur and old, dry stones.

he Scortas resumed their miserable life in Montepuccio. All four of them lived cramped together in the only room in Raffaele's house. Each had found a job and brought home something to eat, but not much more. Raffaele was a fisherman. He did not own his boat, but every morning, at the port, someone would take him aboard for the day, in return for a portion of the day's catch. Domenico and Giuseppe hired themselves out as farmhands. They picked tomatoes or olives. Cut wood. Spent entire days in the heat, bending over an earth that yielded nothing. As for Carmela, she cooked for the other three, took care of the washing, and did a bit of embroidery for people in town.

They hadn't touched what they called amongst themselves "the New York money." For a long time they thought this money should be used to buy a house. For the moment, they had to tighten their belts and wait, but as soon as an opportunity presented itself, they would buy. They had enough to buy something quite respectable, since in Montepuccio, at the time, stone was still worth nothing. Olive oil was more precious than acres of rock.

One evening, however, Carmela looked up from her bowl of soup and declared:

"We have to do things differently."

"What?" asked Giuseppe.

"The New York money. We have to use it for something other than a house."

"That's ridiculous," said Domenico. "Where would we live?"

"And if we bought a house," retorted Carmela, who had already spent hours thinking about this, "you would keep on sweating like animals for the rest of your God-given days, just to earn your daily bread. That would be all you'd have to depend on. And the years would go by. No, we have money; we have to buy something better."

"Like what?" asked Domenico, intrigued.

"I don't know yet. But I'll come up with something."

Carmela's argument had set the three brothers thinking. She was right. There was no doubt about it. Buy a house, and then what? If only they had enough to buy four houses, but that wasn't the case. They had to think of something else.

"Tomorrow is Sunday," continued Carmela. "Take me out with you. I want to see what you see, do what you do, all day long. I'll watch and I'll figure something out."

Once again, the men didn't know what to say. Women in Montepuccio didn't go out, or if they did, it was only at very specific times. In the morning, very early, to go to market; to hear the Mass—though since the death of don Carlo this was no longer the case; and at harvest time, when they came out to pick olives. The rest of the time, they stayed home, cloistered behind the thick walls of their houses, away from the sun and the covetous glances of men. What Carmela was suggesting went against the grain of village life, but ever since their return from America, the Scorta brothers had complete confidence in their little sister's instincts.

"All right," said Domenico.

The next day, Carmela put on her best dress and went out, escorted by her three brothers. They went to the café and drank strong coffee—which wrenched the guts and made the heart beat fast—as was their Sunday custom. Then they sat at a table along the sidewalk and played cards. Carmela was there too, sitting up straight in her chair, a bit off to the side. She watched the men go by. She observed village life. Next, they went to visit a few fishermen friends. At dusk, they went for a *passeggiata**along the Corso Garibaldi, strolling up and down the avenue, greeting people they knew, hearing the day's gossip. For the first time in her life, Carmela spent a whole day in the streets of the village, in a world of men who stared at her in astonishment. She heard comments behind her back. People wondered what she was doing there. They made remarks about how she was dressed. But she didn't care and concentrated on her mission. That evening, when they got home, she carefully took off her shoes. Her feet ached. Standing over her, Domenico watched her in silence.

"So?" he finally asked her. Giuseppe and Raffaele looked up and fell silent so as not to miss a word of her answer.

"Cigarettes," she answered calmly.

"Cigarettes?"

"Yes. We should open a tobacco shop in Montepuccio."

Domenico's face lit up. A tobacco shop. Of course. There weren't any in Montepuccio. The grocer sold a few cigarettes, and you could find them at the market-place, but a real tobacco shop, no, she was right, Montepuccio didn't have one. Carmela had observed the doings of the men during the day, and the only thing the fishers of the old town had in common with the bourgeois of the Corso was that they were all puffing avidly on small cigarettes. In the shade at the hour of aperitifs, or in the heat of the sun as they toiled, they smoked. This was something to work with. A tobacco shop. On the Corso. Carmela was sure of it. A tobacco shop. You could bet your life on it. It would never be empty.

he Scortas set about acquiring the property they wanted. They purchased a commercial space on Corso Garibaldi, a large, empty room of about thirty yards square at street-level. They also bought the basement for storage. After that, they had nothing left. The night of their purchase, Carmela was gloomy and silent.

"What's wrong?" asked Domenico.

"We have nothing left to buy the licence," answered Carmela.

"How much is it?" asked Giuseppe.

"It doesn't cost much, but we'll need some money to butter up the director of the licence bureau. To send him gifts, every week, until he grants us the license. And we don't have enough for that."

Domenico and Giuseppe were dismayed. This was a new, unforseen obstacle, and they did not know how to overcome it. Raffaele looked at the three of them and said to them softly:

"I have some money, and I want to give it to you. The only thing I ask is that you don't ask where it came from. Or how long I've had it. Or why I've never mentioned it before. I've got it. That's all that matters."

He laid a wad of crumpled bills on the table. It was Father Bozzoni's money. Raffaele had sold the watch. Until this day he had always carried the money on him, not knowing what to do with it, not daring either to get rid of it or to spend it. The Scortas shouted for joy, but he felt no relief. Bozzoni's crazy silhouette was still dancing in his head, twisting his guts with remorse.

With Raffaele's money, they set to work on getting the licence. Every two weeks for the next six months, Domenico would leave Montepuccio to go to San Giocondo by donkey. There was an office of the State Monopolies there.* He would bring the director prosciutto, *caciocavallo* cheese, and a few bottles of *limoncello*.* He went back and forth tirelessly. All the money went to buy these delicacies. Six months later, the authorization was granted. The Scortas were finally in possession of a licence. But they had nothing left. Not one lira. Just the walls of an empty room and a little piece of paper that gave them the right to work. There wasn't even enough left over to buy cigarettes. They got their first crates of cigarettes on credit. Domenico and Giuseppe went to fetch them in San Giocondo. They loaded everything onto the donkey's back and, on the way home, for the first time in their lives, it seemed to them that something was finally starting to happen. All they had done up until then was endure their fate. Choices had been made for them. For the first time, they were going to fight for themselves, and this prospect made them smile for joy.

They laid the cigarettes down on cardboard crates. They stacked up the cartons. The place looked like a contrabander's outfit: no counter, no cash register, nothing but the merchandise on the floor. The only thing that indicated that it was an official sales outlet was the wooden sign they had hung over the door, on which was written *Tabaccheria Scorta Mascalzone Rivendita no. 1.** Montepuccio had its first tobacco shop. From that day forward, they would dive heart and soul into a life of sweat that would break their backs and kill them with exhaustion. A life without sleep. The fate of the Scortas would be bound to the boxes of cigarettes they unloaded from the donkey's back early in the morning, before the workers got to the fields and the fishermen returned from the sea. Their whole life was bound to the little white sticks that men held tightly between their fingers and the wind slowly consumed on mild summer nights. A life of sweat and smoke, which was just beginning. A chance to escape from the misery to which their father had condemned them. *Tabaccheria Scorta Mascalzone Rivendita no. 1.*

e stayed on Ellis Island for nine days. We were waiting for a boat to be chartered for the return. Nine days, don Salvatore, to contemplate the country that was forbidden us. Nine days at the gates of paradise. That was the first time I thought back on the moment when my father came home after his night of confession and ran his hand through my hair. Now it seemed that a hand was passing through my hair again, the same hand as before. My father's hand. The hand of the cursed winds of the hills of Apulia, calling me back home. It was the dry hand of misfortune that, since the beginning of time, has condemned whole generations to remain simple clods, living and dying under the sun, in a land where the olive trees are more coddled than the people.

We boarded the ship home. The embarkation wasn't at all the way it was in Naples, with all the confusion and shouting. This time we took our seats in silence, walking slowly, like convicts. The dregs of the earth got on that boat. The sick from all over Europe. The poorest of the poor. It was a ship of sadness and resignation. A boatload of the luckless, the damned, returning home with the endless shame of having failed. The interpreter hadn't lied, the crossing was free. In any case, no one could have afforded a return ticket. If the authorities didn't want beggars piling up on Ellis Island, they had no choice but to arrange the return trips themselves. On the other hand, there was no way they could charter one boat for every country or destination. That ship of rejects crossed the Atlantic and, once in Europe, slowly put in at all the main ports, one by one, unloading its human cargo.

It was a long journey, don Salvatore, endless. The hours passed the way they do in a hospital, to the slow drip of the IV. People were dying in the dormitories, from sickness, disappointment, and solitude. Abandoned by everyone and everything, those creatures had a hard time finding a reason to live they could grasp onto. Often they let themselves drift into death with a vague smile on their faces, happy, deep down, to put an end to the series of trials and humiliations that had been their lives.

Strangely enough, I got stronger. My fever broke. Soon I could cross the deck from end to end. I raced up and down the stairs, I wended my way through the corridors. I was all over the place, going from one group to the next. In a few days, everybody knew me, regardless of their age or language. I spent my days doing little favors, darning socks, finding a little water for the old Irishman, or someone to trade a blanket for a small silver medal that a Danish woman was willing to part with. I knew everyone by name, or surname, at least. I wiped the brows of the sick. I prepared food for the elderly. People called me "the little one." I got my brothers involved. I told them what to do. They moved sick people out onto the deck on sunny days. They passed out water in the dormitories. We were alternately messengers, merchants, nurses, and confessors. Little by little, we managed to improve our lot. We earned a few pennies, won a few privileges. Where did the money come from? Most of the time, from the dead. Many people died. It was understood that the few possessions the dying left behind would go to the community. It would have been hard to do otherwise. Most of the poor creatures were going back to a country where no one was waiting for them. They had left their loved ones behind in America or in lands where they had no intention of returning. Were we to send the few coins they hid in their rags to an address where they would never arrive? The booty was redistributed on board. Often the crew helped themselves to it first. That's where we came in. We made sure the crew was informed as late as possible, and we divided things up in the darkness of the hold. This involved long negotiations. If the deceased had family on board, everything went to the survivors, but if not—which was more often the case—we tried to be fair. Sometimes we would spend hours reaching an agreement on the inheritance of three pieces of string and a pair of shoes. I never tended a sick person with the idea of his impending death in mind or how I might profit from it. I swear it. I did it because I wanted to fight, and this was the only way I had found to do so.

I looked after on an old Polish man in particular, whom I liked a lot. I never succeeded in pronouncing his full name, Korniewski or Korzeniewki, I just called him "Korni." He was small and wizened. He must have been about seventy. His body slowly abandoned him. People had discouraged him from making the trip, from trying his luck. They told him he was too old, too weak, but he had insisted. He wanted to see this land that everyone was talking about. His strength had begun to wane from the start. He kept the smile in his eyes, but he was losing weight by the day. Sometimes he would murmur things in my ear that I couldn't understand, but he made me laugh because the sounds he made seemed like anything but a language.

Korni. He saved us from the poverty that was eating away at our lives. He died before we reached England. He died one night when the ship was gently rocking. The moment he felt himself fading, he called me to his side and handed me a little rag tied with string. He said something I didn't understand, then, letting his head fall back on the bed, eyes wide open, he began to pray, in Latin. I prayed with him, until the moment death robbed him of his last breath.

In the rag there were eight gold coins and a small silver crucifix. That was the money that saved us.

Shortly after old Korni's death, the boat began to put in at the ports of Europe. First it berthed in London, then cast anchor in Le Havre, and then set off again for the Mediterranean, where it stopped at Barcelona, Marseilles and, finally, Naples. At each of these ports of call, the boat discharged its bedraggled passengers and was reloaded with merchandise. We took advantage of these stops to do a little business. The ship would dock at each port for two or three days, enough time for the cargo to be loaded and for the crew to sober up. We used these precious hours to buy a few things, such as tea, pots and pans, cigarettes. We would choose what was most typical of each country and then try to resell them at the next stop. It was a ridiculous business for laughable sums of money, but we carefully amassed a tiny treasure. And we arrived in Naples richer than when we had set out. That's what matters, don Salvatore. I'm proud of this. We came back richer than when we'd left. I discovered that I had a gift, a talent for business. My brothers couldn't get over it. It was that small treasure, wrung from squalor and resourcefulness, that kept us from dying like animals in the teeming crowds of Naples when we returned.

V

THE BANQUET

*N*ight had fallen. Carmela pulled down the metal shutter. She didn't want to be disturbed. "I'm sure there'll be a few late clients," she said to herself, "but with a bit of luck, when they see the grate half-lowered, they won't insist." Anyway, if they called or knocked, she was determined not to answer. She had something important to do. She went behind the counter and nervously picked up the wooden box that served as a cash register. "All things considered, the amount should be in here," she thought. She opened the box, sinking her fingers into the multitude of small, crumpled bills, trying to put them in order, flatten them, and count them, diving into that mass of paper with the frantic eagerness of the poor. There was anxiety in her movements. She was dreading the verdict. Would there be enough? Normally she would wait till she got home to count her earnings without any rush. She would know, at a glance, whether it had been a good or bad day, and she was never in a hurry to confirm the exact amount of cash. Tonight, however, things were different. Tonight she hunched over her cash-box, in the half-light of the shop, like a thief over his loot.

"Fifty thousand lire," she finally murmured when a small, orderly pile of bills stood before her. She took the stack and put it in an envelope, then poured the rest of the box's contents into the cloth money-bag that she used to carry each day's receipts.

Only then did she close the shop, with the swift and nervous movements of a conspirator.

She did not take the road back home. She turned onto the Via dei Martiri and walked at a brisk pace. It was ten past one in the morning. The streets were empty. When she got to the square in front of the church, she noticed with satisfaction that she was the first to arrive. She chose not to sit on one of the public benches. She barely had the time to take a few steps, when at last a man approached. Carmela felt like a little girl standing in the wind. She greeted him courteously, nodding her head. She was nervous. She didn't want this meeting to drag on, since she was afraid someone might see them at that odd hour and people would start to gossip. She pulled out the envelope she'd prepared and handed it to the man.

"There you are, don Cardella. As agreed."

The man smiled and slid the envelope into the pocket of his linen trousers.

"Aren't you going to count it?" she asked in surprise.

The man smiled again, as if to say he had no need for such precautions, then took his leave and vanished.

Carmela stood there, in the square. The whole thing had taken only a few seconds. Now she was alone. It was all over. This rendezvous that had obsessed her for weeks—this deadline that had robbed her of sleep for whole nights at a time—had just taken place without there being anything in the evening breeze or the sounds of the streets to mark this moment in any particular way. Yet she could feel it; her fate had just taken a new turn.

The Scortas had borrowed a great deal of money to keep the tobacco shop afloat. They hadn't stopped running up debts since they first embarked on this adventure. It was Carmela who saw to the finances. Without telling her brothers, she had fallen prey to the vicious circle of usury. In those days, creditors in Montepuccio plied their trade rather simply. One came to an agreement as to the sum, the rate of interest, and the date of reimbursement. On the appointed day, one brought the money. There was no paper, no contract. No witnesses, either. Only one's word and one's faith in the good will and honesty of the other. Woe to anyone who did not repay his debts. The wars between families were bloody and endless.

Don Cardella was Carmela's last creditor. She had turned to him a few months earlier to pay back the money she had borrowed from the owner of the café on the Corso. Don Cardella was her very last resort. He had helped her out of a jam, and in return he got back more than twice the amount he had lent to her. But that was the rule, and Carmela had no complaints.

She watched the silhouette of her last creditor disappear around the corner, and she smiled. She felt like shouting and dancing. For the first time, the tobacco shop was theirs. For the first time, it belonged to them by rights. The risks of repossession were receding. No more mortgages. From now on, they would be working for themselves. Every lira earned would be a lira for the Scortas. "We have no more debts," she murmured, and she repeated this sentence until she began to feel dizzy. It was like being free for the first time.

She thought of her brothers. They had worked hard and generously. Giuseppe and Domenico had taken care of the stonework, remade the floor, whitewashed the interior. Little by little, year after year, the shop had taken shape and come to life. As if that cold space, made of old stones, needed human sweat in order to blossom. The more they worked, the better the tobacco shop looked. People feel these things. Whether it's a shop, a field, or a boat, there is a dark bond between a man and his tool, and it is made of respect and hatred. You take care of it. You lavish endless attention on it, and you revile it at night. It wears you out. It breaks you in two. It robs you of your Sundays and your family life, but nothing in the world could ever make you part with it. This was how things were between the Scortas and their tobacco shop. They cursed it and worshiped it all at once, the way one worships what puts food on the table and curses what makes one age prematurely.

Carmela thought of her brothers. They had sacrificed their time and their sleep, and that was one debt she knew she would never be free of. A debt nothing could ever repay.

She couldn't even share her present happiness with them, for that would have meant talking about the debts she'd incurred, the risks she'd taken, and she didn't want to do that. Yet she couldn't wait to be with them. Tomorrow, on Sunday, she would see them all. Raffaele had sent out a strange invitation a week earlier. He had come by to tell her that he was summoning the whole clan—women, children, everyone—to a place called Sanacore. He did not reveal the reason for the invitation. But tomorrow they would all meet there. She promised herself she would look after her family with greater care than ever, do something for each one of them. She would shower affection on all those whose time she had taken. Her brothers. Her sisters-in-law. All those who, to make the tobacco shop survive, had given a bit of their strength.

When she arrived in front of her house, before pushing in the door and greeting her husband and two sons, she went into the cavelike structure adjacent to it, which they used as a stable. The old donkey was there, in the warm air of the windowless room. The same donkey that had brought them back from Naples. They had never wanted to get rid of him. They used him to transport cigarettes from San Giocondo to Montepuccio. He was a tireless old beast. He'd adapted perfectly to the skies of Apulia and his new life—to the point, indeed, that the Scortas had taught him to smoke. The good animal loved to do it, and the spectacle was a source of delight for the children of Montepuccio and San Giocondo. Whenever they saw him coming, they would run alongside him, yelling "*È arrivato l'asino fumatore! L'asino fumatore!*"* And the donkey did, in fact, smoke. Not cigarettes from the tobacco shop—that would have been casting pearls before swine and, anyway, the Scortas were tight-fisted with every one of their cigarettes. No, along the road they would pull up long, dry weeds, tie them into a bundle the thickness of a finger, and light it. The donkey would puff on it as he walked, in perfect serenity, blowing the smoke out his nostrils. When the shaft shortened and grew too hot, he would spit out the butt haughtily, which always made them all laugh. For this they named him "Muratti,"* the smoking donkey of Montepuccio.

Carmela patted the animal's flanks, whispering in his ear, "Thank you, Muratti. Thanks, *caro*. You sweated for us, too." The donkey gently yielded to her caresses as though he understood that the Scortas were celebrating their freedom and that workdays, henceforth, would never again weigh heavy with the backbreaking weight of servitude.

hen Carmela went into the house, she took one look at her husband and immediately knew he was unusually agitated. For a moment she thought he'd found out that she'd borrowed money from don Cardella without asking for his approval, but that wasn't it. His eyes glistened with a childish elation, not with the ugly glow of reproach. She gazed at him, smiling, and understood, before he had even opened his mouth, that he must be excited about some new project.

Her spouse, Antonio Manuzio, was the son of don Manuzio, a lawyer and town councillor. A rich Montepuccio notable, owner of hundreds of hectares of olive trees, don Manuzio was one of those who had repeatedly had to suffer the pillages of Rocco Scorta Mascalzone. Several of his men had even been killed. When he'd learned that his son wanted to marry the criminal's daughter, he ordered his son to choose between his family and that "whore." He'd used the word *puttana*, which on his lips was as shocking as a stain of tomato sauce on a white shirt. Antonio made his choice and married Carmela, cutting himself off from his family and giving up the leisurely bourgeois life that awaited him. He married Carmela, with no property and no money. Only a name.

"What's on your mind?" Carmela asked, so that

Antonio could have the pleasure of saying what he was dying to tell her.

Face lighting up with gratitude, Antonio shouted, "Miuccia, I have an idea, and I've been thinking about it all day. Actually, I've been thinking about it a long time, but today I'm suddenly sure of it and I've made my decision. It came to me when I was thinking about your brothers."

Carmela's face darkened slightly. She didn't like it when Antonio started talking about her brothers. She would rather he spoke more often about his own sons, Elia and Donato, but he never did.

"So, what is it?" she asked again, a note of weariness in her voice.

"We need to branch out," Antonio replied.

Carmela said nothing. She knew what her husband was about to say to her. Not in detail, of course, but she sensed that it was going to be one of those ideas she could never go along with, and this made her sad and sullen. She'd married a man with a head full of wind and a glint in his eye, but who strolled through life like a funambulist. The thought dampened her spirits and put her in a bad mood. But Antonio was already off and running, and now she would have to listen to him explain everything.

"We need to branch out, Miuccia," he resumed. "Look at your brothers. They're right. Domenico has his café. Peppe and Faelucc' have their fishing. We have to start thinking beyond those damned cigarettes."

"Tobacco is the only thing suitable for the Scortas," Carmela replied laconically.

Her three brothers had married, and all three, at the moment of their marriages, had embraced new lives. One fine day in June, 1934, Domenico had wedded Maria Faratella, daughter of a well-to-do family of merchants. It was a passionless marriage, but it brought Domenico a comfort he'd never known before. For this he felt a gratitude towards Maria that was something like love. With Maria, he was sheltered from poverty. The Faratellas didn't exactly live in luxury, but they owned—aside from several olive groves—a café in Corso Garibaldi. By now Domenico divided his time between the tobacco shop and the café, depending on where he was needed most on a given day. As for Raffaele and Giuseppe, they had married fishermen's daughters, and, ever since, work at sea required the better part of their time and strength. Yes, her brothers had drifted away from the tobacco shop, but such was life. The fact that Antonio used their example to call this change of destiny "branching out" irritated Carmela. It seemed false to her, almost dirty.

"Tobacco is a cross to bear," resumed Antonio, as Carmela remained silent. "Or it will become one if we don't try to change. You did what you had to do, and you did it better than anyone, but now we need to think about evolving. You make money with your cigarettes, but you'll never have what really matters: power."

"What do you suggest?"

"I'm going to run for mayor."

Carmela couldn't suppress a laugh.

"And who will vote for you? You wouldn't even have your own family's support. Domenico, Faelucc', and Peppe. That's it. Those are the only votes you could count on."

"I know," said Antonio, who felt hurt, like a child, though he knew she was right. "I need to show people what I'm capable of. I've already thought of that. These ignorant Montepuccians don't know a thing about politics and are unable to recognize a man's worth. I need to win their respect, and that's why I'm going to go away."

"Where?" asked Carmela, surprised by such determination on the part of her boyish husband.

"To Spain," he replied. "The Duce needs some good Italians ready to give up their youth to crush the Reds. I'm going to be one of them. And when I return, covered with medals, they'll see in me the man they need as mayor, believe me."

Carmela fell silent. She'd never heard any mention of this war in Spain, nor of any of the Duce's plans in that part of the world. Something inside her told her that it was no place for the men in her family. Some sort of visceral premonition. The Scortas' real battle was being fought right here, in Montepuccio, not Spain. On that day in 1936, as on every day of the year, they needed the whole clan to be present. The Duce and his war in Spain could summon other men. She looked at her husband a long time and merely repeated, in a soft voice:

"Tobacco is the only thing suitable for the Scortas."

But Antonio wasn't listening. He'd made up his mind and his eyes were already twinkling, like a child dreaming of distant lands.

"For the Scortas, perhaps," he said. "But I'm a Manuzio. And you are, too, ever since I married you."

Antonio Manuzio had made up his mind. He was determined to leave for Spain, to fight alongside the Fascists. He wanted to complete his political education and embrace this new adventure.

He further explained, late into the night, why this was a brilliant idea and how, upon his return, he would inevitably benefit from the aura of the hero. Carmela wasn't listening. She fell asleep as her boyish husband went on about Fascist glory.

The following morning she woke up in a panic. She had a thousand things to do. Change, dress the two children, fix her hair up in a bun, make sure that the white shirt that Antonio had selected was well-pressed, pomade Elia's and Donato's hair and douse them with cologne so that they would look as beautiful as shiny new coins. And remember her fan, for it was a hot day and the air would soon become stifling. She was in the sort of nervous state one gets in before the children's First Communion or one's own wedding. There were so many things to do. Not forget anything. Try not to be late. She was running from one end of the house to the other, a brush in her hand and a hairpin between her lips, looking for shoes and cursing her dress, which seemed to have shrunk and was hard to button up.

At last the family was ready to leave. Antonio asked yet again where they were supposed to gather, and Carmela repeated, "Sanacore." "Where is he taking us?" Antonio asked, worried. "I don't know," she replied. "It's a surprise." And so they left, leaving behind the heights of Montepuccio and taking the coastal route to the place of that name. There they turned onto a narrow smuggler's trail that led them to a sort of embankment overlooking the sea. They stayed there awhile, undecided, no

longer knowing which way to go, when they spotted a
wooden sign on which were painted the words *Trabucco
Scorta*, and which pointed to a staircase. At the bottom
of an interminable descent, they came to a vast wooden
platform, hanging from the cliff-face and suspended
over the waves. It was one of the many *trabucchi* that still
dot the Apulian coastline, fishing platforms that look
like great wooden skeletons, clusters of time-whitened
planks that hang from the rock and look as if they would
never survive a storm. Yet, there they are and there
they've always been. Hoisting their tall masts over the
water. Resisting the wind and the rage of the waves.
They were formerly used to catch fish without going out
to sea. But they've since been abandoned and are now
nothing more than strange lookout posts that give onto
the water as they creak in the wind. One would think
they'd been constructed haphazardly, yet these unsteady
towers of wooden planks can stand up to anything. On
the platform itself one finds a jumble of ropes, cranks,
and pulleys. When the men put it to work, the whole
thing creaks and strains. The *trabucco* raises its nets
slowly, majestically, like a tall, thin man plunging his
hands in the water, then pulling them slowly back up as
though they held the treasures of the sea.

This *trabucco* belonged to the family of Raffaele's
wife. The Scortas knew this. Until now, however, it had
always been an abandoned structure that nobody used
anymore. A heap of boards and worm-eaten poles. Several months earlier, Raffaele had begun restoring the

trabucco. He would work on it in the evening after a day of fishing, or on days when the weather was bad. But always in secret. He worked on it furiously, and to help him through those moments when he felt discouraged by the immensity of his task, he would think of what a surprise it would be for Domenico, Giuseppe, and Carmela to discover this utterly new, accessible place.

The Scortas couldn't get over it. Not only was there a strange sense of solidity about that heap of old wood, but it had all been decorated with taste and charm. They were even more surprised when they went further inside and discovered, at the center of the platform, amidst the ropes and nets, a great, majestic dining table covered with a fine white tablecloth embroidered by hand. From one corner of the *trabucco* came the scent of grilled fish and bay laurel. Raffaele stuck his head out of a recess in which he'd installed a wood-fired oven and grill, and with a broad smile across his face, he yelled: "Sit yourselves down! Welcome to the *trabucco*! Sit down!" In response to every question people asked as they embraced him, he gave a conspiratorial laugh. "When did you build that oven?" "Where did you find this table?" "You should have told us to bring something." Raffaele would smile and say only, "Sit down, don't worry about anything. Make yourselves at home."

Carmela and her family were the first to arrive, but no sooner had they sat down than they heard some loud shouting from the staircase. It was Domenico with his wife and two daughters, followed by Giuseppe, his wife, and little Vittorio, their son. They were all there. They kissed and embraced. The women complimented each other on the elegance of their outfits. The men traded cigarettes and tossed their nieces and nephews in the air, the little ones screaming with delight in the grips of these giants. Carmela sat apart from the rest for a moment, just long enough to contemplate the reunion of their small community. Everyone she loved was there, radiant in a Sunday light in which the color of the women's dresses caressed the whiteness of the men's shirts. The sea was soft and pleasant. She smiled a rare sort of smile, the kind that shows confidence in life. Her eyes drifted over each one of them. Over Giuseppe and his wife Mattea, the daughter of a fisherman who, in his personal vocabulary, had replaced the word "woman" with the word "whore," so that it was not uncommon to hear him greet a female friend in the street with a resounding "*Ciao puttana!*" to the laughter of the passersby. Carmela's gaze came softly to rest on the children: Lucrezia and Nicoletta, Domenico's two daughters, in their beautiful white dresses; Vittorio—Giuseppe and Mattea's boy—whose mother would give him her breast, murmuring: "Drink, little fool, drink, it's all yours"; and Michele, the most recent member of the clan, wailing in his diapers as the women passed him around. She gazed at them all and told herself that they could all be happy one day. Simply happy.

She was roused from her thoughts by the voice of Raffaele, who was shouting, "Everyone to the table! Everyone to the table!" So she got up and did what she had resolved to do. Look after her family. Laugh with them, embrace them, lavish attention on them. Be there for each in turn, gracefully, happily.

There were fifteen of them at the table. They all looked at one another for a few seconds, surprised at how much the clan had grown. Raffaele glowed with happiness and gourmandise. He had long dreamed of this moment. Everyone he loved was there, at his place, on his *trabucco*. He kept running from one corner to the other, from the oven to the kitchen, the fishing nets to the table, without respite, making sure that everyone was served and wanted for nothing.

This day remained etched in the Scortas' memories. For every one of them, adults as well as children, it was the first time they had ever eaten this way. Uncle Faelucc' had really done things right. For the *antipasti*, Raffaele and Giuseppina brought some ten different dishes to the table. There were mussels as big as your thumb, stuffed with a mixture of eggs, bread and cheese. Fried anchovies. Marinated anchovies whose flesh was firm and melted in your mouth. Octopus tentacles. A salad of tomato and chicory. A few thin slices of grilled eggplant. People passed the dishes from one end of the table to the other. Everyone dug in, happy not to have to choose, happy they could eat it all.

Once the platters were empty, Raffaele brought two enormous, steaming bowls to the table. The first contained a traditional pasta dish typical of the region, *troccoli* in squid ink; the other, a seafood risotto. The dishes

were greeted with a general hurrah that made Giuseppina, the cook, blush. It was one of those moments
when one's appetite seems endless and it's as if one
could keep eating for days. Raffaele also set down five
bottles of local wine, a sharp red wine, dark as the blood
of Christ. The heat was now at its zenith. The guests
were protected from the sun by a straw mat over their
heads, but they could tell, from the searing air, that the
lizards themselves must be sweating.

Conversations arose amidst a din of cutlery, interrupted at moments by a child's question or a spilt glass
of wine. They spoke of everything and nothing. Giuseppina recounted how she'd made the pasta and risotto, as
if it were an even greater pleasure to talk about food as
one was eating. People chatted. People laughed. Each
looked after his neighbor, making sure his plate was
never bare.

When the big platters were empty, everybody felt
sated. Their bellies were full, and they felt good. But Raffaele hadn't made his final statement yet. Next, he
brought out five huge platters filled with every manner
of fish caught that same morning. Sea bass, bream, and
more. A bowl full of fried calamari. Big pink shrimp
grilled over a wood fire. Even a few langoustines. At the
sight of these dishes, the women swore they wouldn't
have any. It was just too much. They would die. But they
had to do justice to Raffaele and Giuseppina; and not
only to them. They had to do justice to life, which was
being offered them through this banquet, which they
would never forget. In southern lands one eats with a

kind of frenzy and piggish gluttony. For as long as one can. As if the worst was yet to come. As if it might be the last time one ate. One must eat as long as the food is there. It's a kind of panic instinct. Too bad if one gets sick from it. One must eat with joy and to excess.

The fish platters made the rounds and people partook with a passion. They no longer ate for their stomachs but for their palates. Yet no matter how hard they tried, they didn't manage to finish the fried calamari. Which left Raffaele in a state of dizzy delight. As far as he was concerned, there must always be some food on the table, otherwise it meant the guests hadn't had enough. At the end of the meal, Raffaele turned to Giuseppe and, patting his brother's stomach, asked, "*Pancia piena?*" Everyone laughed, unbuckling their belts or pulling out fans. The heat had subsided, but their sated bodies were beginning to sweat from all the food they'd wolfed down, all that joyous mastication. Raffaele then brought out coffee for the men and three bottles of *digestivi*: one of grappa, one of limoncello, and one of laurel liqueur. When all had been served, he said to them:

"You all know that the townsfolk call us 'the silent ones.' Because we're the Mute's children, they say that our mouths are only good for eating, never for speaking. All right, then. Let's be proud of it. If that's what keeps the busybodies and bumpkins away, then let's hear it for silence. But let's have the silence be for them, not for us. I haven't lived through all that you've lived through. I'll probably die in Montepuccio without ever seeing any of

the world except for the dry hills around here, but here
is where you are. You. And you know a lot more things
than I do. Promise me you'll talk to my children. That
you'll tell them what you've seen, so that what you
gained from your trip to New York won't die with you.
Promise me that each of you will tell my children one
thing, something you've learned, a memory, a bit of
knowledge. Let's all do that for each other, uncles to
nephews, aunts to nieces. Tell a secret you've kept to
yourself that you'll never tell anyone else. Otherwise our
children will become like all the other Montepuccians,
knowing nothing about the world, knowing only silence
and the heat of the sun."

The Scortas concurred. Yes, let it be so. Let each of
us speak, at least once in his life, to a niece or a nephew.
Tell them what we know before we die. Speak for once to
give advice, to pass on knowledge. To be something
more than mere beasts, living and dying under this
silent sun.

The meal was over. Four hours after they had sat
down to eat, the men were leaning back in their chairs,
the children had gone off to play among the cables, and
the women started clearing the table.

They were all exhausted now, as after a battle.
Exhausted and happy. For the battle, that day, had been
won. They had taken pleasure in a bit of life, together.
They had escaped the harshness of their days. The meal
lived on in everyone's memory as the great banquet of
the Scortas. It was the only time the whole clan was

gathered in full. If the Scortas had had a camera, they would have immortalized that afternoon of sharing. They were all there. Parents and children. It was the family's apogee. It should all have remained that way.

Yet it wouldn't be long before things fell apart, before the ground beneath their feet began to crack and the women's pastel dresses darkened with the grim shade of mourning. Antonio Manuzio would go off to Spain and die there from a bad wound—without glory or fanfare—leaving Carmela a widow with her two sons. This would be the first pall cast over the family's happiness. Domenico, Giuseppe, and Raffaele would decide to leave the tobacco shop to their sister—since it was all she had, with two other mouths to feed—so that Elia and Donato wouldn't start out with nothing, and so they wouldn't know the kind of poverty their uncles had known.

Misfortune would soon undermine the busy lives of these men and women. For the moment, however, nobody gave it a thought. Antonio Manuzio poured himself another glass of grappa. They basked in their happiness under the generous gaze of Raffaele, who wept for joy to see his brothers savoring the fish he had grilled himself.

At the end of the meal, they all had full bellies, dirty fingers, stains on their shirts and sweat on their brows. But they were blissful. They left the *trabucco* with regret and went back to their everyday lives.

For a long time, the warm and powerful scent of grilled laurel remained, for them, the scent of happiness.

ow you know why I shuddered when I realized, yes-terday, that I had forgotten Korni's name. If I forget this man, even for a second, it's because everything is falling apart. I haven't finished my story yet, don Salvatore. I need a little more time. Just relax and smoke.

When we got to Montepuccio, I made my brothers swear never to talk about our failure in New York. We let Raffaele in on our secret the night we buried the Mute because he'd asked us to tell him about our trip and none of us wanted to lie. He was one of us. He also swore not to tell. They have all kept their word. I didn't want anyone to know. As far as Montepuccio is concerned, we went to New York and we lived there for a few months. Long enough to make a little money. When people asked us why we came back so soon, we answered that it wasn't right to leave our mother here alone. We had no way of knowing she was dead. That was enough. People didn't ask any more than that. I didn't want them to know that the Scortas hadn't been allowed into the country. What counts is what people say, the stories they tell about you. I wanted New York to be part of the Scortas' story. For us to stop being a family of degenerates and paupers. I know the people here. They would have said that bad luck dogs our steps. They would have brought up Rocco's curse. There's no shaking off that *sort of thing. We came back richer than when we set out. That's all that matters. I've never said anything about this to my sons. None of the children know. I made my brothers swear to it, and they have kept their word. Everyone had to believe in New York. And we did even better than that. We talked about the city and our life there. In detail. We could do this because old Korni had done the same for us. On the return trip, he found a man who spoke Italian and asked him to translate his brother's letters for us. We listened to him for nights on end. I still remember some of them. Korni's brother talked about his life and the neighborhood he lived in. He described the streets, the people in his building. Korni had these letters read to us, and it was not another torment like the rest. He opened the doors of the city to us. We walked around. We settled there in our minds. I told my sons about New York, and this was thanks to old Korni's letters. Giuseppe and Domenico did the same. That's why I brought you the "Naples-New York ex-voto," don Salvatore. I want you to hang it in the nave. A one-way ticket to New York. I want it to hang in the church of Montepuccio. I want candles to be lit for old Korni. It's a lie. But you do understand, don't you, that it's really not? You'll do as I ask. I want Montepuccio to keep believing that we were there. When Anna is old enough, you can take it down and give it to her. She'll ask you questions and you'll answer them. In the meantime, I want the Scortas' eyes to shine with the sparkle of the great city of glass.*

VI

THE SUN-EATERS

One morning in August 1946, a man entered Montepuccio on a donkey's back. He had a long, straight nose and small, dark eyes. A face not without nobility. He was young, perhaps twenty-five, but his long, gaunt face gave him a severity that made him look older. The oldest folks in town thought of Luciano Mascalzone. The stranger walked with the same slow pace of destiny. Maybe he was some descendant. He went straight to the church, however, and, before even emptying his bags, feeding his mount, or washing himself, before even drinking a little water or stretching his limbs, to the whole town's amazement he pealed all the bells at full force. Montepuccio had her new priest: don Salvatore, whom the people did not take long to dub "the Calabrian."

The very day of his arrival, don Salvatore celebrated Mass before three old women who had entered the church out of curiosity. They wanted to see what the newcomer was like. They were stunned and immediately spread the rumor that the young man had delivered a ferocious sermon. This intrigued the Montepuccians. The following day, five more people came, and so on until the first Sunday, when the church was full. Whole families showed up. They all wanted to see if the new priest was the right man for the job, or if he would suffer a similar fate as his predecessor. Don Salvatore did not seem the least bit intimidated. When it came time for the sermon, he began speaking with authority:

"You call yourselves Christians, and you come seeking comfort from our Lord because you know He is good and just in all things. But you enter His house with dirty feet and foul breath. And I'm not talking about your souls, which are black as ink. Sinners, you are. Born sinners, as we all are, yet you wallow in this state, the way a pig wallows in mud. There was a thick layer of dust on the benches in this church when I entered a few days ago. What kind of village is this, that lets dust cover the house of Our Lord? And I don't want to hear about your poverty. I don't want to hear about the fact that you have to work day and night in the fields, which leaves you so little time. I come from a land where your fields would be considered the Garden of Eden. I come from a land where the poorest man among you would be considered a prince. No. Admit it, you have lost your way. I know about your peasant ceremonies. I can tell just by looking at your ugly faces. Your exorcisms. Your wooden idols. I know about your outrages against the Almighty, your profane rites. Admit it, and repent, you band of brutes. The Church can offer you forgiveness and make you into something you've never been before: good and honest Christians. The Church can do this, because she is good to her own. But you're going to have to do it through me, and I've come here to make your life impossible. If you persist in your disgraceful ways, if you shun the Church and scorn her priest, if you keep on indulging in your primitive rites, just listen what will happen to you, and do not doubt it for an instant: the heavens shall cloud over and it shall rain for thirty days and thirty nights. The fish will shun your nets. The olive trees will grow from the roots down. Your donkeys will give birth to blind cats. And before long there will be nothing left of Montepuccio. For this shall be the will of God. Pray for His mercy. Amen."

The congregation was dumbfounded. At first some grumbling could be heard. People quietly protested. Then, little by little, silence returned—a rapt, admiring silence. Outside the church, the verdict was unanimous: "He's got guts, this guy. Not like that candy-ass from Milan."

Don Salvatore was adopted. They'd liked his solemnity. He had the harshness of the Southern lands and the dark gaze of men who know no fear.

A few months after his arrival, don Salvatore had to face his first baptism of fire: preparing the feast of Sant'Elia, the town's patron saint. For a whole week, he couldn't sleep. The day before the festivities, he was still running from one place to the next, brows knit. The streets were decked out for the celebration. Paper lanterns and garlands had been hung. The next morning, at the crack of dawn, several cannonblasts shook the walls of the houses. Everything was ready. The excitement increased. Children grew restless. The women were already preparing the menu for the feast days. They were frying, one by one, in the sweat of their kitchens, slices of eggplant for the parmigiana. The church had been decorated. The wooden statues of the saints had been brought out and displayed for the parishoners: Sant'Elia, San Rocco, and San Michele. They were covered with jewelry, as tradition demanded: gold medals and chains, offerings that sparkled in the glow of the candles.

At eleven o'clock in the evening, while all of Montepuccio was out on the Corso, peacefully sampling the cool drinks and ice cream, a wild yell rang out and don Salvatore appeared, livid, eyes rolling back as if he'd just seen the devil, lips pale, on the verge of fainting. With a voice that sounded like the wail of a wounded animal, he cried, "Somebody has stolen the medals of San Michele!" All at once, the whole town fell silent. The silence lasted long enough for each of them to grasp in full what the priest had said. The medals of San Michele. Stolen. Here. In Montepuccio. It wasn't possible.

Then, all of a sudden, the silence turned into a dull rumble of anger, and the men all stood up. Who? Who could have committed such a crime? It was an insult to the whole town. Nobody could remember such a thing ever happening. To rob San Michele! On the eve of the celebration! It would bring bad luck to everyone in Montepuccio. A group of men went into the church. They questioned those who had come to pray. Had they seen any strangers prowling about the place? Or anything out of the ordinary? They looked everywhere. They checked to make sure the medals hadn't fallen at the foot of the statue. Nothing. Nobody found anything. Don Salvatore kept repeating, "Damn! Damn! This town is a pack of criminals!" He wanted to cancel everything. The procession, the Mass, everything.

At Carmela's house, the consternation was as great as everywhere else. Giuseppe had come over for dinner. All during the meal, Elia never stopped squirming in his chair. When, at last, his mother removed his plate, he exclaimed:

"Ha! Did you see the look on don Salvatore's face!"

And he broke into a strange laughter that made his mother turn pale. She understood at once.

"Was it you? Elia? Was it you?" she asked, her voice cracking.

The boy started laughing even harder, with that mad laughter the Scortas knew so well. Yes, it was him. Quite a prank, one had to admit. What a look on don Salvatore's face! What panic, all over town!

Carmela was ashen. She turned to her brother and said in a weak voice, as though she were dying:

"I'm going out. Kill him."

She got up and slammed the door. She went straight to Domenico and told him everything. Giuseppe, for his part, let his anger well up inside him. He thought of what the townsfolk would say. He thought of the shame that would be heaped on the family. When he finally felt his blood boiling, he stood up and gave his nephew a thrashing such as no uncle had ever done before. He opened a gash in the boy's eyebrow and split his lip. Then he sat down beside him. His wrath had subsided but he felt no relief. A tremendous gloom filled his heart. He'd beaten the child, but in the end the result was the same. There was no way out. Then, turning towards his nephew's swollen face, he said:

"That was an uncle's rage. Now I leave you to the town's rage."

He was about to go out, leaving the boy to his fate, when he remembered something.

"Where'd you put the medals?" he asked.

"Under my pillow," replied Elia between sobs.

Giuseppe went into the boy's room, slid his hand under the pillow, pulled out the pouch in which the thief had hidden his treasure and, mortified, head hanging and eyes dead, went straight to the church. "The feast of Sant'Elia should still take place, at least," he said to himself. "Too bad if they tear us apart for spawning such a heathen. But the feast should still take place."

Giuseppe hid nothing. He woke don Salvatore and, without giving him time to regain consciousness, handed him the medals, saying, "Don Salvatore, here are the saint's medals. There's no point in hiding the criminal's name from you. God knows already. It's my nephew, Elia. If he survives the beating I just gave him, all he'll have left to do is make his peace with the Lord after the Montepuccians get through with him. I'm not asking you for anything. No favors, no leniency. I just wanted to bring you back the medals. The feast should take place tomorrow, as it has every twentieth of July in Montepuccio since the beginning of time."

Then, without waiting for an answer from the priest—who sat there, stunned, torn between joy, relief, and anger—he turned around and went home.

Giuseppe was right to think that his nephew's life was in danger. Without anyone's knowing how, the rumor that Elia Manuzio was the faithless thief had begun to spread. Groups of men had already gathered, vowing to deal the blasphemer a beating he would never forget. They looked for him everywhere.

The first thing Domenico did when his sister showed up in tears was to go get his pistol. He was determined to use it if anyone stood in his way. He went straight to Carmela's, where he found his nephew half-unconscious. He picked him up and, without even taking a moment to wash his face, put him on the back of one of his mules and took him to a small stone hut in the middle of his olive groves. He threw him down on a straw bed, and let him drink a little. Then he locked him in for the night.

The next day, the feast of Sant'Elia took place as usual. Nothing of the previous day's drama was visible on people's faces. Domenico Scorta took part in the festivities, as was his wont. He carried the statue of San Michele in the procession and told whoever wanted to listen that his degenerate of a nephew was a wretch and that, if he wasn't afraid to spill his own blood, he would kill him with his bare hands. Nobody suspected for a moment that he was the only person who knew where Elia was hiding.

The following day, groups of men went out again in search of the criminal. Although the most important things had been salvaged—they'd been able to celebrate Mass and hold the procession—the thief still needed to be punished, and in exemplary fashion, so that this would never happen again. They hunted for Elia for ten whole days. They looked for him all over town. In the middle of the night, Domenico would slip out and secretly bring him provisions. He didn't talk. Or he spoke very little. He only gave him food and drink. Then he would leave, always taking care to lock him back in. After ten days, the searches ceased and the village calmed down. But for Elia to go back to Montepuccio was unthinkable. Domenico found him a place at the house of an old friend in San

Giocondo, a father with four sons who all worked hard in
the fields. They arranged for Elia to stay there a year, and
only after that year could he return to Montepuccio.

Once they'd loaded some things on the donkey's
back, Elia turned to his uncle and said, "Thank you, *zio*,"
his eyes full of repentance. At first his uncle said
nothing. The sun was rising over the hills. A fine rosy
light caressed their ridges. Then he turned to his nephew
and spoke words that Elia would never forget. In the
beautiful light of the dawning day, he revealed to Elia
what he considered his own personal wisdom:

"You are nothing, Elia. Me neither. All that matters is
the family. Without it, you'd be dead, and the world
would keep on turning without even noticing you were
gone. We're born, we die, and in the time in between,
only one thing matters. You and me alone, we're nothing.
But the Scortas, the Scortas, that's something. That's why
I helped you out. No other reason. From now on, you
have a debt. You're indebted to the people with the same
name as you. One day, say, twenty years from now, you'll
pay off this debt. By helping one of our own. That's why
I saved you, Elia. Because we're going to need you when
you become a better man—the same way we're going to
need every one of our sons. Never forget that. You're
nothing. The Scorta name passes on through you. That is
all. Now go, and may God, your mother, and the townsfolk forgive you."

*H*is brother's exile made Donato as melancholy as a feral child. He no longer spoke, no longer played. He would stand for hours in the middle of the Corso without moving, and when Carmela would ask him what he was doing, he always answered, "I'm waiting for Elia."

The solitude that had suddenly been imposed on his playtime had turned his world upside down. Without Elia around, life became ugly and boring.

One day, sitting in front of his mug of milk, Donato looked at his mother in wide-eyed seriousness and asked, "Mama?"

"Yes," she answered.

"If I steal the medals of San Michele, can I go join Elia?"

Carmela felt horrified by the question. Dumbfounded. She rushed to her brother Giuseppe's place and recounted the scene to him.

"Peppe," she added, "you have to look after Donato, or he'll end up committing a crime. If he doesn't die of sadness first. He doesn't want to eat anymore. He only talks about his brother. Take him away with you somewhere, make him smile. A boy his age shouldn't have dead eyes. The child has drunk of the world's sorrows."

Giuseppe did as he was told. That very evening, he took his nephew to the harbor and onto his boat. When Donato asked where they were going, Peppe answered that it was high time he understood a thing or two.

The Scortas dealt in contraband. They always had. They had started during the war. The rations-coupons represented a serious restriction on business. The fact that only a limited number of packs of cigarettes could be sold per inhabitant seemed preposterous to Carmela. She started with the English soldiers, who willingly traded a few cartons for some prosciutto. The trick was to find soldiers who didn't smoke. Then Giuseppe was put in charge of the traffic with Albania. Boats would come ashore at night, full of cigarettes stolen from government warehouses or other tobacco shops in the area. The clandestine cartons cost less and allowed them to maintain a cash-box that escaped fiscal controls.

Giuseppe had decided to let Donato take his first journey as a smuggler. To the slow rhythm of the oars, they set out for the Zaiana cove. A little motorboat was waiting for them there. Giuseppe greeted the man, who spoke poor Italian, and they loaded ten cases of cigarettes onto their boat. Then, in the calm night that had settled over the water, they returned to Montepuccio without exchanging a word.

When they put in at the port, something unusual

happened. Little Donato did not want to go ashore. He stayed in the boat, looking determined, arms crossed.

"What's wrong, Donato?" asked his uncle, amused.

The little boy looked at him long and hard, then asked in a steady voice:

"Do you do this often, *zio*?"

"Yes," answered Giuseppe.

"Always at night?"

"Always at night," the uncle answered.

"And that's how you make money?" asked the child.

"Yes."

The child was silent for a while longer. Then, in a voice that allowed no reply, he declared:

"That's what I want to do, too.'

This nocturnal voyage had filled him with happiness. The sound of the waves, the darkness, the silence: there was something mysterious and sacred about it, and this had overwhelmed him. Traveling by boat, drifting with the current. Always at night. Secrecy as profession. To him this all seemed fabulously free and bold.

On the way home, impressed with his nephew's infatuation, Giuseppe took him by the shoulders and said, "You have to get by, Donato. Remember that. You have to get by. Don't let anybody tell you it's illegal, forbidden, or dangerous. The fact is, you have to take care of your own. That's all there is."

The child remained pensive. This was the first time that his uncle had talked to him this way, in such a serious tone. He heard him and, not knowing what to answer to the rule that had just been proclaimed, he remained silent, proud to see that his uncle thought he could talk to him like a man.

*D*omenico was the only person who saw Elia during his year of exile. While for everyone else the theft of the medals of San Michele had been a stinging slap in the face, for Domenico it was an opportunity to discover his nephew. There was something about the prank that appealed to him.

On the anniversary of the theft of the medals of San Michele, Domenico paid an unannounced visit to the home of the family that was lodging Elia, asked to see him and, when he appeared, took him by the arm and went walking with him in the hills. Uncle and nephew talked together, following the slow cadence of their steps. At the end, Domenico turned to Elia and handed him an envelope, saying:

"Elia, if all goes well, in a month you should be able to return to the village. I think people will take you back. Nobody talks about your crime anymore. They've calmed down. And there's going to be another feast of Sant'Elia. If you want, you can be back with us in a month. But I came to propose something different to you. Here, take this envelope. There's money in it, a lot of money, enough to live on for six months. Take it and leave. Go wherever you want. Naples, Rome, Milan. I'll send you more if what's in there isn't enough. I want you to understand me, Elia. I'm not sending you away. But I

want you to have a choice. You could be the first Scorta
to leave this land. You're the only one capable of it. Your
theft is proof. You've got nerve. Your exile has made you
grow up. That's all you need. I haven't told a soul about
this. Your mother doesn't know a thing. Nor do your
uncles. If you decide to go away, I'll explain everything
to them. Now listen, Elia, listen to me: you have one
more month. I'm leaving you the envelope. I want you
to think it over."

Domenico kissed his nephew on the forehead and
embraced him. Elia was dumbfounded. So many desires
and fears crowded together inside him. The Milan train
station. The big cities up north, enveloped in clouds of
factory smoke. The lonely life of the emigrant. His mind
could not find its way through this jumble of images.
His uncle had called him a Scorta. What did he mean by
that? Or had he simply forgotten that his last name was
Manuzio?

One month later, at an hour when the morning light
was beginning to heat up the rocks, there was a knock
on the door of Domenico's fine old house. Domenico
went to open the door. Elia stood before him, smiling.
He immediately handed him the envelope with the
money for the trip.

"I'm staying," he said.

"I knew you would," his uncle replied in a soft voice.

"How?" asked Elia.

"The weather is too good right now," said Domenico.
Since Elia didn't understand, he motioned for him to

come in, gave him something to drink and explained. "The weather is too good. For the last month the sun has been beating down hard. It was impossible for you to leave. When the sun rules the sky, so hot it splits the rocks, you can't do anything. We love this land too much. It gives nothing, it's even poorer than we are, but when the sun heats it up, none of us can leave. We're born of the sun, Elia. We have its heat inside us. As far back as our bodies can remember, it was there, warming our skins when we were babies. And we never stop eating it, crunching it with our teeth. It's there in the fruits we eat, the peaches, the olives, the oranges. It's in the scent. When we drink the oil, it slides down our throats. It's inside us. We are the sun-eaters. I knew you wouldn't leave. If it had rained these past few days, maybe. But when it's like this, not a chance."

Elia listened to Domenico's rather grandiose theory with amusement, as if to show that he only half believed it. His uncle was happy and wanted to talk. It was his way of thanking Elia for having returned. Then the young man began to speak in turn:

"I came back for you, *zio*. I don't want to learn of your death by a long-distance telephone call and to cry, alone, in some room in Milan. I want to be here, by your side. To learn from you."

Domenico listened to his nephew with sadness in his eyes. Of course he was thrilled with Elia's decision. Of course he had prayed for many nights that the young man would choose not to leave. But something inside him considered this return a capitulation. It reminded him of the New York failure. Never, therefore, would a Scorta be able to leave this miserable land. Never would a Scorta escape from the sun of Apulia. Never.

When Carmela saw her son with Domenico beside him, she crossed herself and thanked heaven. Elia was here. After being away for more than a year. He was walking confidently down the Corso, and no one blocked his path. There wasn't a whisper. Not one dark look. No groups of men forming behind him. Montepuccio had forgiven him.

Donato was the first to rush into Elia's arms, shouting for joy. His big brother had come home. He was eager to tell him about everything that had happened during his absence: the nocturnal sea voyages, the smuggling, the hiding places for the crates of illegal cigarettes. He wanted to tell him everything, but for the moment he was happy just to squeeze him in his arms, in silence.

Life resumed in Montepuccio. Elia worked with his mother at the tobacco shop. Donato asked his uncle Giuseppe every day if he could come with him, and was so insistent that the good man ended up making a habit of taking him along every time he went out to sea at night.

Whenever he could, Elia would go visit Domenico on his lands. The oldest Scorta was aging slowly as the summers passed. This hard, closed man had turned into a gentle soul with blue eyes and a certain noble beauty

about him. He had developed a passion for olive trees
and succeeded in realizing his dream of owning several
hectares of them. What he loved most was to contemplate the hundred-year-old trees when the heat subsided
and the sea breeze rustled their leaves. All he cared about
anymore was his olive trees. He always said that olive oil
would save the South. When he watched the liquid flow
slowly out of the bottles, he could not help smiling in
contentment.

When Elia visited him, he would always invite the
boy to sit on the big terrace. He would send for a few
slices of white bread and a bottle of his own olive oil,
and they would partake of that nectar reverentially.

"It's pure gold," the uncle would say. "People who
say we're poor have never eaten a crust of bread soaked
in oil at our house. It's like biting into these hills. It tastes
like the rocks and the sun. It glistens. It's beautiful, thick,
smooth. Olive oil is the blood of our land. And people
who treat us like peasants have only to look at the blood
that flows in our veins. It is sweet and generous. Because
that's what we are: purebred peasants. Poor wretches
with sun-wrinkled faces and calloused hands, but who
look you straight in the eye. Look at all the parched land
around us, and savor the richness of this oil. Between
the two, there's human labor, and you can taste that in
our oil, too. Yes, you can taste the sweat of our people,
the calloused hands of our women who picked the
olives. And it's noble. That's why it's good. We might be
poor and uncouth, but we've made oil out of rocks,
we've made so much from so little, and for this we shall

be saved. God will recognize our effort. Our olive oil will answer for us."

Elia remained silent. This terrace overlooking the hills, this terrace where his uncle loved to sit, was the only place he felt alive. He could breathe here.

Domenico went into town less and less. He preferred to sit in a chair in the middle of a grove and stay there, in the shade of an olive tree, watching the sky change color. But there was one appointment he would not miss for anything in the world. Every summer evening, at seven o'clock, he would meet his two brothers, Giuseppe and Raffaele, on the Corso. They would go to a café, always the same one, *Da Pizzone*, where their table awaited them outside. Peppino, the owner of the café, would join them, and they'd play cards from seven o'clock to nine o'clock. These meetings were sacred. They would drink San Bitter or artichoke liqueur, slamming their cards down on the wooden table, laughing and shouting. They would raise their voices, calling each other all kinds of names, cursing the heavens when they lost a round, thanking Sant'Elia or the Madonna when they were on a winning streak. They would tease each other gently, taunt the unlucky one, slap one another on the back. They basked in their happiness. Yes, in those moments they lacked nothing. Peppino would bring out more drinks when the glasses were empty and recount a bit of local gossip. Giuseppe would call out to the neighborhood kids, who all called him *zio* because he always gave them coins to go buy grilled almonds. They played cards as if time no longer existed. They would sit there at their outdoor table, in the wondrous sweetness of those summer evenings, perfectly at home. Nothing else mattered.

One day in June, Domenico didn't show up at *Da Pizzone* at seven o'clock. Raffaele and Giuseppe waited a while. In vain. They sensed that something serious had happened. They rushed to the tobacco shop to see if Elia had seen his uncle. Nothing. So they ran to his property, knowing, deep down, that the worst was yet to come. They found their brother seated in a chair, in the middle of the olive grove, arms dangling, head slumped onto his chest, hat on the ground. He had died. Calmly. A warm breeze softly tossed a few locks of his hair. The olive trees around him protected him from the sun and surrounded him with a soft rustling of leaves.

"Ever since Mimì died, I can't stop thinking about something."

Giuseppe had spoken softly, without raising his head. Raffaele looked at him, waiting to see if the rest of the sentence would follow, then, noting that Giuseppe was not forthcoming, he asked gently:

"About what?"

Giuseppe hesitated a moment, then got it off his chest.

"When have we been happy?"

Raffaele looked at his brother with a sort of compassion. Domenico's death had left Giuseppe unexpectedly shaken. After the funeral he had suddenly aged, losing the lifelong plumpness that had made him look like a young man, even in his later years. Domenico's death had sounded the knell, and from that moment on, Giuseppe kept himself ready, knowing instinctively that he would be next. Raffaele asked his brother:

"Well? What's *your* answer to the question?"

Giuseppe remained silent, as if he had a crime to confess. He seemed to hesitate. "That's just it," he said shyly. "I've been thinking. And I've tried to make a list of the happiest moments I've known."

"Are there many?"

"Yes, many. At least I think so. Enough. The day we bought the tobacco shop. Vittorio's birth. My wedding.

My nephews. My nieces. Yes. There are quite a few."

"So why do you seem so sad?"

"Because when I try to pick one, the happiest memory of all, do you know what keeps coming to mind?"

"No."

"The day you invited us all to the *trabucco* for the first time. That's the one that keeps coming up. The banquet. We ate and drank like we were blessed."

"*Pancia piena*?" laughed Raffaele.

"Yeah, *pancia piena*," repeated Giuseppe, tears in his eyes.

"What's so sad about that?"

"What kind of man," replied Giuseppe, "declares at the end of his life that his happiest day on earth was the day of a meal? Aren't there happier moments in a man's life? Isn't that the sign of a miserable life? Shouldn't I be ashamed of myself? Yet, I assure you, every time I think about it, that's the memory that comes to mind. I remember everything. There was the seafood risotto that melted in your mouth. Your Giuseppina wore a sky-blue dress. She was as beautiful as could be, rushing back and forth between the table and the kitchen. I remember you, at the oven, sweating like a miner. And the sound of fish sizzling on the grill. You see? After a whole life, that's the best memory of all. Doesn't that make me the most miserable man in the world?"

Raffaele had listened quietly. His brother's voice had let him relive that meal, let him see again that joyous gathering of Scortas: the dishes passing from hand to hand, the happiness of eating together.

"No, Peppe," said his brother. "You're right. Who can boast that they've known such happiness? Not too many of us. Why disdain it? Because we were eating? Because it smelled of fried food and our shirts were stained with tomato sauce? Happy are those who shared this meal. We were together. We ate, we talked, we shouted and drank like men. Side by side. Those were precious moments, Peppe. And I would give anything to savor them all over again. To hear your booming laugh and smell grilled laurel again."

*D*omenico was the first to go, but Giuseppe did not survive him by much. The following year he had a bad fall in the old town and lost consciousness. The only hospital in the Gargano was in San Giovanni Rotondo, a two-hour drive from Montepuccio. Giuseppe was put in an ambulance that raced off into the hills, sirens wailing. The minutes passed slowly, like a knife over skin. Giuseppe was getting weaker. After forty minutes on the road, the ambulance was still a tiny dot in the rocky expanse. Giuseppe suddenly came to and had a moment of lucidity. He turned to the medic and said to him, with the determined voice of a dying man:

"I will be dead in half an hour. You know it's true. In half an hour. I can't hold on any longer. There's not enough time to get to the hospital. So turn around and drive as fast as you can. You still have time to get me back to my village. That's where I want to die."

The two medics took these words to be the expression of a last will and did as they were told. The ambulance turned around in the parched expanse of hills, then resumed its mad course towards Montepuccio, sirens still wailing. It got there in time. Giuseppe had the satisfaction of dying in the main square, surrounded by his loved ones, who were dumbfounded by the return of this ambulance that had thrown in the towel in the face of death.

Carmela wore mourning for the rest of her days. She did for her brothers what she hadn't done for her husband. Raffaele was inconsolable. It was as if someone had cut the fingers off his hand. He wandered about the village, not knowing what to do with himself. All he could think about was his brothers. He would go back to *Da Pizzone* every day and say to his friend, "Let's join them soon, Peppino. They are both there and we're here, and nobody can play cards anymore."

He went to the cemetery every day and talked to the shadows for hours on end. One day he brought his nephew, Elia, and decided to talk to him in front of the two uncles' graves. He had put off this moment for a long time, convinced that he, who had never traveled, had nothing to teach anyone. But he had promised to do this. Time was passing, and he did not want to die without keeping his word. So there, in front of the graves, he rested his hand on the nape of Elia's neck and said to him:

"We were no better or worse than anyone else, Elia. But we tried. That's all. We tried with all our might. Every generation tries to build something, to consolidate their possessions or to make them grow. To take care of their own. Everybody does his best. All you can do is try. But don't expect anything at the end of the race. Do you know what there is at the end of the race?

Old age, nothing else. So listen, Elia, listen to your old uncle Faelucc', who doesn't know anything about anything and never went to school. Make the most of the sweat of your brow. That's all I have to say. Because those are the best moments in life. When you're fighting for something, when you're working day in and day out like a poor devil and you don't have time to see your wife and children, when you sweat to build what you want, you're living the best moments of your life. Believe me. Your mother, your uncles and I cherished nothing so much as the years when we didn't have a cent to our name, nothing, when we were fighting for the tobacco shop. Those were hard years. But for every one of us, those were the best moments of our lives, building from scratch, hungry as wolves. Make the most of the sweat of your brow, Elia. Remember that. After that, it's all over so fast. Believe me."

Raffaele had tears in his eyes. Speaking of his two brothers and the luminous years when they had lived together, sharing everything, moved him like a child.

"Are you crying?" asked Elia, who was touched by the sight of his uncle in such a state.

"Yes, *amore di zio*,"* answered Raffaele, "but it's all right. Believe me, it's all right."

As I said, don Salvatore, I was in debt to my brothers, deeply in debt. I knew it would take years to pay it all off, maybe my whole life. I didn't care. It was like an obligation. But what hadn't occurred to me was that I might, one day, stop wanting to pay it back. I had sworn to myself to give them everything. Work my whole life long and give them what I'd saved. It was the least I could do for them. I swore to myself I would be a sister and only a sister. And that's what I did, don Salvatore. I was a sister my whole life long. My marriage didn't change a thing. The proof is that when people hear of my death, they won't say, "Manuzio's widow is dead." Nobody knows who Manuzio's widow is. They'll say, "The Scortas' sister died." Everyone will know that's me, Carmela. I'm happy that things are this way. That's who I am. Who I've always been. A sister to my brothers. Antonio Manuzio gave me his name but I didn't want it. Is it shameful to admit that? I never stopped being a Scorta. Antonio merely passed through my life.

The only happiness I've ever known was when I was surrounded by my brothers. My three brothers. When we were together, we could devour the world. I thought things would continue like that, up until the end. I lied to myself. Life went on, and time took it upon itself to *change everything, little by little. It made me a mother.*

    We all had children. The clan got bigger. I didn't realize that would change everything. My sons were born. I was a mother. From that day on I became a she-wolf, like all mothers. What I built, I built for them. What I earned, I earned for them. I kept everything for Elia and Donato. A she-wolf, don Salvatore, who thinks only of her young and bites anyone who comes near. I had a debt, and it remained unpaid. But I would have had to take from my sons to repay my brothers. Who could ever do such a thing? I did what any mother would have done. I forgot my debt and I fought for my brood. I can see by your expression that you almost forgive me. That's basically what mothers do, you're thinking. It's normal to give everything to one's children. I ruined my brothers, don Salvatore. I prevented them from leading the lives they dreamed of. I forced them to leave America, where they would have made a fortune. I drew them back to these southern lands that offered nothing. I had no right to forget that debt. Not even for my children.

    Domenico, Giuseppe, and Raffaele. How I loved those men. I am a sister, don Salvatore. But a sister who, for her brothers, was only the unsightly face of misfortune.

VII

TARANTELLA

*L*ittle by little, Carmela abandoned the tobacco shop. At first she started coming in less and less often, then not at all. Elia took her place. He would open and close up shop, do the accounts, and spend his days behind the counter where his mother, before him, had used up her life. He would get bored the way dogs get bored on hot days. What else could he do? Donato categorically refused to spend even a single day in the shop. He'd agreed to work for the business on one sole condition, which was non-negotiable: that he be allowed to continue his back-and-forth journeys as a smuggler. The business that had been the center of the family's activity for so long was now like a hot potato to those in charge of it. Nobody wanted any part of it. Elia had resigned himself to taking his place behind the counter, but only because he had nothing better to do. Every morning he would chide himself for being incapable of anything else.

After living this life for a while, he became strange. He was often distracted, quick to anger. He would stare at the horizon with a dark look in his eye. He seemed to spend the day selling his packs of cigarettes without even noticing what he was doing. One day, Donato took advantage of a moment when they happened to be alone

to ask his brother: "What's wrong, *fra*?"* Elia looked at
him with surprise, shrugged his shoulders, and frowned.
"Nothing," he said.

So convinced was Elia that nothing in his behavior
betrayed his inner turmoil, that he was stunned by his
brother's question. What had he said, what had he done
that might make Donato think that anything was
wrong? Nothing. Absolutely nothing. He hadn't said
anything. He hadn't done anything he didn't normally
do. All he did was sell those blasted cigarettes, spending
the whole day behind that goddamned counter, serving
those goddamned customers. This life filled him with
horror. He felt on the verge of a major upheaval, like an
assassin the night before his crime. But he had repressed
his anger, his need to strike out, deep inside himself,
hiding it from everyone like a secret plotter, and when
his brother had asked him simply, "What's wrong,
brother?", he'd felt as if he'd been unmasked, stripped
naked. And that only increased his anger.

The truth was that Elia was in love with Maria
Carminella. The girl was from a rich family that owned
the Grand Hotel Tramontane, the finest in Montepuccio. Maria's father was a doctor. He divided his
time between his patients and managing the hotel. Elia
would feel his blood begin to boil whenever he walked
past the four-star hotel. He would curse its vast swim-
ming-pool, its curtains that flapped in the wind, its
enormous restaurant with a view of the sea, its plot of
beach dotted with red and gold deckchairs. He cursed all
this luxury because he knew it was an insurmountable

barrier between him and Maria. He was nothing but a bumpkin, and everybody knew it. He might have a tobacco shop, but that made no difference. It wasn't a question of money, but of inheritance. What did he have to offer the doctor's daughter? To come sweat with him on summer nights, when the tobacco shop was never empty? It was a joke, a lost cause from the start. He had gone over this same argument a thousand times during his sleepless nights. And a thousand times he'd reached the same conclusion: it was better to forget Maria than to expose himself to certain humiliation. Yet, despite this reasoning, despite all these irrefutable arguments, he was unable to forget the doctor's daughter.

Finally, one day, he made up his mind, summoned all his courage, and went to see old man Gaetano Carminella. He'd asked if he could come by late in the morning, and the doctor had courteously replied in his calm voice that it was always a pleasure to see him and that he would wait for him on the terrace of the hotel. At that hour the tourists were already at the beach. Old man Gaetano and Elia were alone, both wearing white shirts. The doctor had ordered two Camparis, but Elia was too worried about what he had to say to touch the drink. After they'd exchanged the customary pleasantries, old man Gaetano began wondering what this young man who said nothing wanted from him. Surely he hadn't come all this way to ask him how his family was doing. At last Elia took the plunge. He'd made and remade the speech a thousand times, weighing each

word, pondering every turn of phrase, but the words
that came out had nothing in common with what he'd
so often repeated to himself. His eyes were flashing. He
looked like a murderer admitting to his crime, who feels,
as he speaks, the sweet euphoria of confession well up
inside him.

"Don Gaetano," he said, "I won't lie to you, and I
want to get right to the point. I have nothing. I own
nothing but that blasted tobacco shop, and it's more like
a cross to bear than a life-saver. I'm poor, and that
damned business only adds to my poverty. Not many
people can understand that. But you, don Gaetano, you
understand, I know you do. Because you're a shrewd
man. That tobacco shop is the crassest, most miserable
thing about me, and it's all I've got. When I come here
and see this hotel, when I walk past your house in the
old town, I realize it's already very generous of you to sit
down with me and hear me out. But in spite of this, don
Gaetano, in spite of this, I want your daughter. She's in
my blood. I've tried to reason with myself, believe me.
Any reason you can come up with for not granting my
request, I've already thought of. I know them all. And
they're justified. I've repeated them to myself over and
over. It's useless, don Gaetano. Your daughter is in my
blood, and if you won't let me have her, something bad
will come of this that will sweep us all away, the
Carminellas and the Scortas together. Because I'm crazy,
don Gaetano. Do you understand? I'm crazy."

The old doctor was a sensible man. He understood
that Elia's last words were not a threat but quite simply

a statement of fact. Elia was crazy. Women can do that to men. It was best not to provoke him. The old man with the white beard and small blue eyes took his time responding. He wanted to show that he was thinking about Elia's request and taking his arguments into consideration. Then, in his calm, town-elder sort of voice, he began speaking about the respect he had for the Scorta family—a courageous family that had pulled itself together by dint of hard work—but he added that, as a father, he had to consider only the best interests of his loved ones. This was his sole concern in life. To look out for the well-being of his daughter and family. He would think over what Elia had said and would give him an answer as soon as possible.

On his way home, Elia went back to the tobacco shop. His head was empty. His confession had brought him no relief. He only felt exhausted. What he didn't know was that as he was walking, head down and brows knit, commotion reigned at the Hotel Tramontane. Once the meeting was over, the women of the house, sensing some amorous intrigue, had pressured Gaetano into revealing the reasons for Elia's visit, and the old man, assailed from all sides, had given in. He told them everything. As of that moment, a whirlwind of shouting and laughter swept over the house. Maria's mother and sisters commented on the qualities and flaws of this surprising suitor. They had the old doctor repeat Elia's speech word for word. "I'm crazy." Did he really say, "I'm crazy"? Yes, Gaetano confirmed. He even repeated it. This was the Carminella family's first marriage request.

Maria was the eldest, and nobody had ever thought the question would arise so soon. While the family was having the story told to them for the thousandth time, Maria slipped out. She wasn't laughing. She was bright red in the face, as if she'd been slapped. She exited the hotel and ran after Elia. She caught up to him as he was about to enter his tobacco shop. He was so surprised to see her, alone and chasing after him, that he just stood there, mouth agape, and didn't greet her. When she was only a few yards from him, she said:

"So, just like that, you come to our place and ask my father for my hand." She looked in the grips of an animal fury. "I guess that's how you go about things in your backward family. Me, you don't ask anything. I'm sure it didn't even occur to you. You say there will be trouble if you can't have me. Well, what have you got to offer me? You cry to my father that you're not rich enough. You talk about hotels, big houses. Is that what you would offer me if you had the means? Is it? A house? A car? Answer me, mule. Is that what you'd give me?"

Elia was taken aback. He didn't understand. The girl was shouting louder and louder. So he muttered, "Yes, that's what I'd give you."

"Well, then, rest assured," she replied with a scornful smile that made her more beautiful and prouder than all the other girls in the Gargano, "rest assured that, even if you owned the Palazzo Cortuno, you would have nothing. I'm more expensive than that. Hotels, houses, cars—I can brush these things away with the back of my hand. Do you hear me? I'm more expensive than that.

Can you understand that, you miserable clod? Much more expensive. I want everything. And I'll take everything."

Having said these words, she turned around and vanished, leaving Elia stunned. At that moment, he knew that Maria Carminella was going to become a ver-itable obsession.

ass had just ended and the last parishioners were coming out in disparate groups. Elia was waiting in front of the church, sad-eyed, arms dangling at his sides. Seeing him there, the priest asked him if everything was all right, and when Elia didn't answer, he invited him out for a drink. When they were settled in at a café table, don Salvatore asked him in a tone that demanded an answer, "What's wrong?"

"I can't take it any more, don Salvatore," replied Elia. "I'm going crazy. I want… I don't know. To do something else. Start another life, leave town, dump that blasted tobacco shop."

"What's stopping you?" asked the priest.

"Freedom, don Salvatore. You have to be rich to be free," replied Elia, surprised that don Salvatore didn't understand this.

"Stop whining, Elia. If you want to leave Montepuccio or go off into I don't know what field, all you have to do is sell the tobacco shop. You know very well that you'd get a good price for it."

"It would be like killing my mother."

"Leave your mother out of this. If you want to go away, then sell. If you don't want to sell, then stop complaining."

The priest said what he thought in that tone of voice which the townsfolk loved so much. He was tough and direct and spared nobody's feelings.

Elia felt he couldn't take the discussion any further without speaking of the real problem, the reason why he was cursing the heavens: Maria Carminella. But he didn't want to talk about that, especially not with don Salvatore. The priest interrupted Elia's thoughts.

"Only on the last day of a person's life can he say whether he's been happy or not," he said. "Until that day, you have to try to look after yourself as best you can. Follow your own road, Elia. That's all you can do."

"Mine doesn't lead anywhere," Elia muttered, thinking hard of Maria.

"That's another matter. It's another matter, and if you don't do anything about it, you'll be guilty."

"Guilty of what? Cursed, that's what I am!"

"Guilty," continued don Salvatore, "of not having lifted your life as high as it could go. Forget about luck. Forget about fate. Make an effort, Elia. Make an effort. See it through. Because so far, you haven't done anything."

With these words, the old man left Elia and disappeared, though not before patting him on the shoulder with his wrinkled, Calabrian peasant-hands. Elia thought about everything that had been said. The priest was right. He hadn't done anything. Nothing at all. The first action he'd ever taken as a man was to go see Gaetano to ask him for his daughter Maria's hand, and even there, he'd gone about it with his head down, as though defeated from the start. The priest was right. Elia hadn't done anything. It was time to make an effort. He sat there alone, on the terrace of *Da Pizzone*. He was absently turning his spoon in his coffee cup, and with each turn, he murmured, as if hypnotized, "Maria, Maria, Maria…"

*A*fter his conversation with don Salvatore, Elia was determined to try his luck again. In any case, he had no choice. He could no longer sleep. He could no longer speak. At the rate things were going, he didn't give himself more than a month before he went completely insane and jumped off the cliffs of Montepuccio into the sea, which never gives back the bodies it takes. He couldn't find a way to be alone with Maria. He couldn't approach her on the beach or in the cafés. She was always surrounded. So he did what murderers and desperadoes do, he started following her one day when she was on her way home from shopping. And when she turned onto a narrow street in the old town, deserted but for a few sleepy cats, he rushed after her like a shadow, seized her by the arm and, eyes rolling as if with fever, he said, "Maria—"

"What do you want?" she cut him off at once, without even flinching, as if she'd sensed he was behind her all along.

Her brusque tone made him lose heart. He hung his head, then looked back up at her. Her beauty was enough to damn one's soul. He felt himself blush, and this only infuriated him further. She was so close, he could touch her. Embrace her. But her gaze condemned him to blushing and stammering. He had to take the plunge. Make an effort. Tell her everything. Too bad if she made fun of him and laughed with the cats in the alley.

"Maria, today I want to talk to you, not your father. You're right. I was a fool. You told me you wanted everything. Do you remember? 'I'll take everything,' you said. Well, I'm here to tell you that it's all yours to take. I'm giving you everything. Down to my last lira. Still, it won't be enough. Others could offer you more, because I'm not the richest of men; but nobody would be ready, like me, to give you everything he owned. I don't want to keep anything. You can have it all."

He was getting worked up as he spoke, his eyes screwed up in an ugly smile. Maria stood stock still, her face immobile, staring at Elia. Her gaze seemed to strip him naked.

"You certainly come from a family of shopkeepers," she said with a scornful grin on her lips. "Money, that's all you know how to offer. Why do you think you can buy me like that? Do I look like a pack of cigarettes or something? You want to buy yourself a wife. The only women you can buy with gold and jewelry are whores or Milanese. That's all you know how to do, buy. Go on, get out of my way. Go find yourself a wife at the cattle market, pay whatever price you want. Me, I'm too expensive for you."

Saying this, she resumed her walk home. In a sudden, unthinking gesture, Elia grabbed her arm. He was livid, lips quivering. Why he'd done this, even he didn't know. But he held her firmly. Two thoughts clashed in his head. One said he should let her go at once, that this whole scene was ridiculous and he should let her go and beg her pardon. But a blinder impulse made him clutch that arm in rage. "I could rape her," he said to himself. "Right here, on this street. Right now. Rape her. It doesn't matter what happens afterward. She's so close. Her arm, here, struggling, but not hard enough. I could take her. It would be one way to have her, at least, since she'll never marry me."

"Let me go."

The order rang in his ears. He let go at once, and before he could recover his senses, before he could smile or beg pardon, she'd disappeared. Her voice had been so firm, so commanding, that he'd obeyed without a thought. Their eyes had met one last time. Elia's were empty, like those of a drug addict or insomniac, and if he'd had his wits about him, he would have seen in Maria's gaze a kind of smile that belied the coldness in her voice. A voluptuous glint had flashed in her eyes, as though the contact of his hand on her arm had succeeded in touching her more than his words. But Elia saw none of this. He stood there in the street, drained of strength, dismayed by the way this exchange, which he'd dreamed about for so long, had turned out.

When the young man burst into the church, don Salvatore was smoking a cigarette, which he did very rarely, but always with profound pleasure. It reminded him of his life in Calabria, before the seminary, when he and his companions, aged twelve, would puff on the cigarettes they'd pinched.

"What's the matter?" asked don Salvatore, frightened by the look on Elia's face.

"I'm finished," replied Elia, and, no longer feeling constrained by modesty, he began for the first time to tell someone about his love. He told the priest everything. The nights he had spent thinking only of this. The obsession. The terror he felt in her presence. Don Salvatore listened for a while, then, when it seemed to him he'd heard enough, he raised his hand to make Elia stop, and said to him:

"Listen, Elia. I can be of help with the dead, because I know the prayers. I can be of help raising children, because I brought up my nieces after my brother died. But when it comes to women, there's nothing I can do."

"But then?" asked Elia, at a loss.

"Well, I'm Calabrian," don Salvatore continued, "and in Calabria, when somebody's eating his heart out for love, he dances the tarantella. Something always comes of it. Something happy or something tragic."

*D*on Salvatore didn't merely advise Elia to dance the tarantella; he also gave him the name of an old woman in the old part of town, a Calabrian who would see to his needs if he showed up at her door at midnight with a tin of olive oil.

Elia did as instructed. One evening, he knocked on the door of a small house. An eternity passed before anyone answered. Finally, a little old woman with a face like a wrinkled apple stood before him. She had piercing eyes and droopy lips. Elia realized he'd never seen her before in the village. She uttered a few words that he didn't understand. It was neither Italian nor Montepuccian patois. Maybe some Calabrian dialect. Not knowing what to reply, Elia held out his tin of oil. The old woman's face lit up. In a shrill voice she said: "Tarantella?", as if the word itself delighted her, and she opened the door.

The house consisted of a single room like the houses of old. There was a straw mattress. A stove. A pail for when nature called. The floor was dry earth. It resembled the house that Raffaele used to have near the port, where the Scortas had lived upon their return from New York. Without saying anything, the old woman put a bottle of liqueur on the table, gestured to him to help himself, and went out of the house. Elia obeyed. He sat down at the table and poured himself a glass. He thought he'd be drinking grappa or limoncino, but this alcohol didn't taste like anything he knew. He emptied his glass and served himself another, hoping to identify the liqueur. It went down his throat like lava and tasted like rocks. "If the stone of the South had a flavor, this would be it," thought Elia, now on his third glass. Could one possibly obtain a juice like this by squeezing the rocks of the hills? Elia let the drink's dense heat sweep through him. He was no longer thinking of anything. The door then opened again, and the old woman reappeared, followed by a man, who was blind and even older than she. Elia had never seen him before either. He was thin and wizened, and as small as the woman. He sat down in a corner and took out a tambourine. The two old-timers then began singing the ancient tarantellas of the land of the sun, and Elia let the age-old chants fill his soul. They told of the madness of men and the bite of women. The little crone's voice had changed; it was now the voice of a virgin, nasal and high-pitched, and it made the walls shake. The old man tapped the ground with his foot as his fingers thumped the tambourine, his own voice joining in with the woman's. Elia poured himself another glass. The liqueur's flavor had changed. It wasn't stone they had pressed to make it; it must have been bursts of sun, the *solleone*, "the lion sun," tyrannical orb of the summer months. The liqueur tasted like the sweat that beads on the backs of men working the fields. It tasted like a lizard's heart, beating rapidly against the rock. It tasted like the earth that splits and cracks as it begs for a little water. The *solleone* and its power as unbending sovereign, that's what Elia had in his mouth.

The little old woman was now dancing in the middle of the room and she invited Elia to join her. He drank a fifth glass and stood up. They began the spider-dance to the rhythm of the chants. The music filled Elia's head. It sounded to him as if there were a dozen musicians in the room, and as the chants crested and ebbed throughout his body, he understood their innermost meaning. His head was spinning and sweat poured down his back. He felt as if his whole life was flowing down to his feet. The crone, who only a few minutes ago had seemed so slow and weary, was now bounding all around him. She was everywhere. She encircled him, never taking her eyes off him. She smiled at him with the wizened ugliness of a fruit gone bad. Now he understood, yes, he understood everything. His blood was heating up, and he understood that this crone, laughing with her toothless mouth open wide, was the face of destiny that had laughed at him so many times before. There she was, feverish and furious. He closed his eyes, no longer following the woman's movements. He was dancing. The repetitive, dizzying music filled him with happiness. He heard in these ancient laments the only truth he had ever known. The tarantella possessed him in full, the way it possesses lost souls. He felt as strong as a giant now. He had the world at his fingertips. He was

Vulcan in his overheated cave. His every footstep gave off sparks. All of a sudden, a voice rose up inside him. It was the old woman's voice. Unless it was the music itself. Or the liqueur. It kept saying the same thing, endlessly repeating itself, to the staccato rhythm of the music:

"Go forth, young man, go forth, the tarantella shall go with you. Do what you must do."

Elia turned towards the door. He was surprised to find it open. It didn't occur to him to turn back toward the two old people. The music was now inside him, resonating with the power of ancient processions.

He walked down the streets of the old town like a man possessed. It was four o'clock in the morning and even the bats were asleep.

Without having actually decided to go there, he found himself in front of the tobacco shop on the Corso. His blood was on fire. He was sweating all over. The world was spinning around him, the crone's voice tickling his ear. Driven by the tarantella biting his heart and sucking his blood, he entered the tobacco shop, went into the storeroom and set fire to a crate of cigarettes. Then, without turning back towards the flames, which were beginning to catch, he went back outside and stood on the sidewalk across the street to enjoy the spectacle. The fire caught fast. Thick smoke poured out of the storeroom. It wasn't long before the flames were attacking the counter. From where Elia was standing, it looked at first as if somebody had turned on the lights.

Then the glow turned more orange in color and the flames appeared, licking the walls and dancing victoriously. Elia shrieked like a madman and started laughing. The Mascalzone spirit was in his veins, and he laughed the laugh of destruction and hatred which his line had passed down from generation to generation. Yes, let it all burn. What the hell. The cigarettes and the money. His life and his soul. Let it all burn. He howled with laughter and, in the glow of the fire, danced to the tarantella's mad rhythm.

The noise of the blaze and the smell of the smoke soon woke the neighbors, who rushed out into the street. Some of them questioned Elia, but since he didn't answer and simply kept staring into space like a madman or simpleton, the men concluded it had been an accident. How could they have imagined that Elia had set fire to the shop himself? They organized themselves and went out in search of extinguishers. A dense crowd squeezed into the street. At that moment Carmela appeared, her face pale, hair disheveled. She looked crazed and could not take her eyes off the blazing spectacle. Seeing the poor woman staggering on the sidewalk, everyone understood it was not just a business that was burning down, but the life and legacy of a whole clan. People's faces were sad the way they are at times of great cataclysms. After a while some charitable neighbors accompanied Carmela back home, to spare her any further exposure to the distressing spectacle of the blaze. It was pointless for her to remain there. It was needless torture.

The sight of his mother had sobered Elia up in a hurry, and his euphoria gave way to profound anguish. He called out to the crowd, shouting to everyone gathered there:

"Do you smell that? Do you smell the smoke? That's the smell of my mother's sweat. Don't you smell it? Her brothers' sweat, too."

The Montepuccians finally brought the flames under control. The fire hadn't spread to the neighboring houses, but there was nothing left of the tobacco shop. Elia was devastated. With the flames extinguished, the spectacle had lost its hypnotic beauty. It was ugly and dismaying. Smoke rose from the stone, black and stifling. He was sitting on the sidewalk. The tarantella had fallen silent. He was no longer laughing. He gazed at the wisps of smoke, wild-eyed.

The townsfolk were already starting to scatter in groups when Maria Carminella appeared before Elia like a ghost. She was in a white dressing gown, her black hair falling onto her shoulders. She walked straight up to him. He still had the strength to stand up. He didn't know what to say. He merely pointed at the smoldering tobacco shop. She smiled at him as she had never done before, and murmured:

"What happened?"

Elia didn't answer.

"The whole thing, gone up in smoke?" she persisted.

"The whole thing," he replied.

"So what have you got to offer me now?"

"Nothing."

"That's good," said Maria. "If you want me, I'm yours."

The days that followed the fire were days of ash and toil. They had to clear away the wreckage, clean up the site, save what could be saved. That thankless task would have finished off the most determined of men. It was enough to make one lose hope. The black walls, the rubble on the floor, the crates of cigarettes gone up in smoke, all this made the shop look like a city razed after a battle. Yet by dint of sheer obstinacy, Elia made it through the ordeal without apparently being affected by it. The truth was that Maria's love swept everything else away. It was all he could think about. The state of the tobacco shop was secondary. He had beside him the woman he had so desired. Nothing else mattered.

Maria did exactly what she had promised. She moved in with Elia. The day after the fire, as they were drinking coffee, Elia declared:

"I didn't sleep at all last night, Maria. And it wasn't because I couldn't stop thinking about the fire. We're going to get married, Maria. You know as well as I do that your father is richer than I'll ever be. You know what people will say? That I married you for your father's money."

"I couldn't care less what people say," Maria replied calmly.

"Me neither. It's myself I'm most worried about."

Maria looked up at her man, puzzled. She didn't understand what he was getting at.

"I know how all this will turn out. I'll marry you. Your father will offer me a job as manager of the Hotel Tramontane, I'll accept, and I'll end up spending summer afternoons playing cards around the pool with my friends. It's not for me. The Scortas are not made for that kind of thing."

"You're not a Scorta."

"Yes I am, Maria. I'm more a Scorta than a Manuzio. I can feel it. That's just the way it is. My mother passed the black blood of the Mascalzones on to me. I'm a Scorta. Who burns down what he loves. You'll see, one day I'll burn down the hotel Tramontane, if I end up owning it."

"You burned down the tobacco shop?"

"Yes."

Maria fell silent a moment. Then she spoke again, softly:

"And what are the Scortas made for?"

"For sweat," replied Elia.

There was a long pause. Maria was contemplating what this all meant. It was as though she could see the future flash before her eyes. With her gaze, and in her mind, she embraced the life that Elia was offering her. Then she smiled gently and, in a proud, haughty tone, she replied:

"Then let's hear it for sweat."

Elia was solemn. As if to assure himself that his woman understood, he continued, "We won't ask anyone for anything, and we won't accept anything. We'll be alone, you and me. I have nothing to offer. I'm a heathen."

"The first thing we must do," she replied, "is clear out the tobacco shop so we can at least store the crates of cigarettes there."

"No," Elia said calmly, smiling. "The first thing we must do is get married."

The wedding took place a few weeks later. Don Salvatore blessed their union. Elia invited all the guests to a great feast at the *trabucco*. Michele, Raffaele's son, had set up a long table amidst the nets and pulleys. The whole family came. The celebration was simple and joyous, the food abundant. At the end of the meal, Donato stood up, relaxed and smiling, asked for silence, and began to speak.

"Today, my brother, you got married," he said. "I see you there in your suit, leaning over your wife's neck to whisper something in her ear. I see you raise your glass to the health of all present, and you look beautiful to me. It's the simple beauty of joy. I wish I could ask life to leave you exactly the way you are now, young and unspoiled, full of desire and strength. To let you pass through the years without changing. Show you none of the ugly faces that life has. I see you here today, and it makes me feel hungry. When times get hard, when I'm bemoaning my fate, when I'm cursing this dog's life of ours, I'll think back on these moments, on your faces glowing with joy, and I will tell myself: Don't curse life, don't bemoan fate. Remember Elia and Maria, who were happy, at least for one day in their lives, and that on this day, you were beside them."

Elia embraced his brother with feeling. At that moment, their two cousins, Lucrezia and Nicoletta, sang an Apulian song, with all the women singing the refrain in chorus: "*Aïe, aïe, aïe / Domani non mi importa per niente / Questa notte devi morire con me.*"* The guests all laughed. The Scortas let these happy hours permeate their souls, and the evening went on in this fashion, in the joy of the cool summer wine.

*I*n the months that followed, a strange thing happened in Montepuccio. Since the late 1950s, the town had two tobacco shops—the Scortas' and another. The two families were fond of each other. There was enough business for everyone, and the spirit of competition never set them against one another. This, however, was not the case with the countless retail outlets that various camping sites, hotels, apartment complexes, and night clubs had opened up. Officially, they were only selling a few packs to bail out their customers, but in certain cases, they actually engaged in illegal sales.

At first, Elia and Maria didn't have the money to do the work required to reopen the shop, and so, in the early going, they sold their cigarettes like street-peddlers.

The strangest thing was that the villagers refused to buy their cigarettes anywhere else. On Sundays, the tourists would watch in astonishment as a long queue of people waited outside the dirtiest, dustiest shop on the Corso. A shop without a sign, counter, or cash register. Just four walls, two chairs, and crates of cigarettes on the floor, into which Elia would thrust his arms to extract packs and cartons. On summer evenings, he would sell them on the sidewalk while Maria, inside, washed the walls. Yet the Montepuccians kept queuing up. Even when Elia would tell them he didn't have their brand of cigarette (since he couldn't buy much, he concentrated on only a few brands), they would actually laugh and say, "I'll take whatever you've got!" and pull out their wallets.

The hand of don Salvatore was behind this surge of solidarity. Day after day, at Mass, he would exhort his flock to help one another. The result far exceeded his hopes.

He was ecstatic to learn that his calls for brotherhood had been taken to heart. Then, one day, passing in front of the tobacco shop and seeing a new sign hanging impressively over the entrance, he let fly:

"I guess maybe these renegades aren't all fit to be cast into Hell."

In fact, the bright new sign had arrived from Foggia that very day. It read: *Tabaccheria Scorta Mascalzone Rivendita no. 1*. To anyone who didn't look closely, the sign might have looked exactly like the one that was there before. The one that Carmela, Domenico, Giuseppe and Raffaele had proudly hung there in their youth. But Elia knew that this one was different. He and the shop had come to a new understanding. The Montepuccians also realized this and now looked at the display window with pride, knowing that they too had played a part in this unexpected rebirth.

Elia's spirit had undergone a profound transformation. For the first time, he was working happily. Never before had circumstances been so harsh. Everything had to be redone. But something had changed. He was no longer inheriting; he was building. He wasn't managing a property handed down to him by his mother; he was struggling with all his might to grant his wife a little comfort and happiness. He was rediscovering, in the tobacco shop, the same happiness his mother had experienced working there. He now understood the obsessiveness and madness with which she spoke of her business. Everything had to be redone. And in order to do this, he had to make an effort. Yes, never before had life seemed so full and precious.

I think often about my life, don Salvatore. What does it all mean? It took me years to build the tobacco shop. Day and night. And when it was finally there, when at last I could pass it on to my sons without worry, it got swept away. Do you remember the fire? Everything burned down. I wept in rage. All my efforts, all my accumulated nights of toil. A simple accident, and it all went up in smoke. I didn't think I could survive it. I know that's what the townsfolk thought as well. Old Carmela won't survive the death of her tobacco shop. I hung on, though. Yes, I stuck it out. Elia set about rebuilding everything from scratch, patiently. It was good. It wasn't entirely my tobacco shop anymore, but it was good. Ah, my sons, I clung to them tight, but here too everything fell apart. Donato disappeared. I curse the sea every day for taking him away from me. Donato. What does it all mean? These lives, built so slowly and patiently, with willpower and self-sacrifice, these lives swept away in one fell swoop by the winds of misfortune—these promises of joy that we dream about, torn apart. Do you know what's most astonishing in all this, don Salvatore? Let me tell you. It's that neither the fire nor Donato's disappearance did me in. Any other mother would have gone mad. Or let herself die. I don't know what I'm made of. I'm hard. I hung on. Without wanting to. Without thinking *about it. I can't help it. There's something inside me that keeps going and won't give in. Yes, I'm hard.*

It was after Giuseppe's funeral that I first stopped talking. I would keep silent for whole hours at a time, then days. You know all this, since you were already here by then. At first, the townsfolk were curious about my new silence. They wondered about it. Then they got used to it. Very soon, for all of you, it was as though Carmela Scorta had never spoken. I felt far away from the world. I had no more strength. Everything seemed useless to me. The town thought Carmela was nothing without the Scortas. They thought she would rather cut herself off from life than go on living without her brothers. They were wrong, don Salvatore. They always are. There was something else that kept me silent all these years. Something I've never told anyone.

A few days after Giuseppe's funeral, Raffaele came to see me. It was a mild day. I immediately noticed that his gaze was clear, as though he'd washed his eyes in pure water. His smile glowed with calm determination. I heard him out. He spoke for a long time, never once lowering his eyes, and I remember every one of his words. He said he was a Scorta, and was proud to have taken this name. But he also said he cursed himself at night. I didn't understand what he meant, but I sensed that my world was about to be turned upside down. I didn't move. I listened. He took a deep breath, then spoke without interruption. He said that the day he buried the Mute, he had wept twice. The first time was in the cemetery, in front of us. He said he *wept because we had honored him by asking him to become our brother. The second time was that evening, in bed. He wept, biting his pillow to avoid making noise. He was crying because by saying yes to us, by becoming our brother, he had also become my brother. And that was not what he had hoped. He paused a moment after saying this. And I remember praying that he would say no more. I didn't want to hear any more. I wanted to get up and leave. But he went on, "I've always loved you." That's what he said, looking me calmly in the eye. But he'd become my brother that day, and he'd sworn to behave like one. He said that because of this, he'd had the pleasure of spending his whole life close to me. I didn't know what to say. Everything was spinning inside me. He went on talking. He said that on certain days he would curse himself like a dog for not having said "no" in the cemetery. "No" to this brother business, and for not having asked for my hand instead, over my mother's grave. But he didn't dare. He said "yes." He took the shovel we handed to him, and he became our brother. "It felt so good to say yes to you," he said. And he added: "I'm a Scorta, Carmela, and I could never say whether I regret it or not."*

He didn't take his eyes off me the whole time he was talking. And when he'd finished, I felt that he was waiting for me to speak in turn. But I remained silent. I felt surrounded by his expectation. I wasn't trembling. I was empty. I couldn't say anything. Not a word. There was nothing inside me. I looked at him. Time had passed. We were face to face. He understood that I wasn't going to respond. He waited a little longer. He was hoping. Then he quietly stood up, and we parted. I didn't say a word. I just let him leave.

From that day on, I remained silent. When we saw each other the next day, we acted as though nothing had happened. Life went on, but I spoke no more. Something had broken. What could I say to him, don Salvatore? Life was already over. We were old. What could I say to him? We should start all over again, don Salvatore. I was a coward. We should start all over, but so many years have gone by.

VIII

THE SINKING SUN

When he felt death approaching, Raffaele summoned his nephew. Donato came, and they both remained silent a long time. The old man couldn't bring himself to begin the conversation. He watched Donato quietly drink the glass of Campari he'd handed him. He almost gave up, but finally, despite his fear that he might encounter a look of disgust or anger in his nephew's eyes, he broke in:

"Donato, do you know why I'm your uncle?"

"Yes, *zio*," Donato replied.

"You were told how we decided to become brothers and sister the day I helped your uncles Mimì and Peppe bury the Mute."

"Yes, *zio*," Donato repeated.

"And how I, in turn, gave up my original family name, which was worthless, so I could carry the name of Scorta."

"Yes, *zio*. That's what I was told."

Raffaele paused briefly. The moment had come. He was no longer afraid. He was anxious to unburden his heart.

"There's a crime I want to confess."

"A crime?" asked the young man.

"Quite a few years ago, I killed a man of the Church. Don Carlo Bozzoni, the priest of Montepuccio. He was a nasty man, but I damned myself by killing him."

"Why did you do it?" asked Donato, stunned by this confession from the man he'd always considered the gentlest of his uncles.

"I don't know," Raffaele muttered. "It just rose up in me all at once. I had this enormous anger inside me, waiting, and it got the better me."

"Why were you angry?"

"I'm a coward, Donato. Don't look at me that way. Believe me, I'm a coward. I didn't have the courage to ask for what I wanted. That's why the anger built up inside me. That's why it exploded in front of that stupid, good-for-nothing priest."

"What are you talking about?"

"Your mother."

"My mother?"

"I didn't have the courage to ask her to marry me."

Donato sat there open-mouthed.

"Why are you telling me this, *zio*?" he asked.

"Because I'm going to die and it will all be buried with me. I want at least one person to know what I've been carrying in the pit of my stomach all my life."

Raffaele fell silent. Donato didn't know what to say. He wondered, for a moment, whether he should reassure his uncle or show some sort of disapproval instead. He felt empty, stunned. There was nothing more to add. His uncle was not waiting for him to respond. He'd spoken to get things out in the open, not to have someone else's opinion. Donato had the feeling this conversation would change him more than he could ever foresee. He stood up, a little embarrassed. His uncle looked at him a long time, and Donato sensed that the old man almost wanted to apologize for having confided in him. As if he would rather have taken these old stories to the grave with him. They embraced warmly and parted.

Raffaele died a few days later, in his nets, on his *trabucco*, with the sound of the sea beneath him, his heart unburdened. At the funeral, his coffin was carried by his son Michele and his three nephews, Vittorio, Elia, and Donato. Carmela was there. Her face was expressionless. She didn't cry. She stood up straight. When the coffin was presented to her, she brought her hand to her mouth and placed a kiss on the wood, and Raffaele smiled in death.

Seeing the coffin pass, everyone in town had the feeling that it was the end of an era. It wasn't Raffaele they were burying, but the whole Scorta Mascalzone family. They were burying the old world. The one that had known malaria and the two wars. The one that had known emigration and poverty. They were burying old memories. People are nothing. They leave no trace. Raffaele was leaving Montepuccio, and as he passed, all the men took off their hats and bowed their heads, knowing that they too, in turn, would soon be gone, and that the olive trees would not weep for them.

*H*is uncle's revelation made Donato's universe totter. Henceforth, he looked at life around him with a kind of weariness in his eyes. Everything seemed false to him. His family history now seemed like a paltry succession of frustrated existences. These men and women had not led the lives they'd wanted. His uncle had never dared declare his love. How many other secret frustrations lay buried in the family's history? An immense sadness came over him. The company of others became unbearable to him. All he had left was the smuggling. He threw himself into it body and soul. He lived on his boat. That was all he could ever be, a smuggler. He attached no importance to the cigarettes; it could just as easily have been jewelry, alcohol, or bags full of worthless paper. The important thing was those nocturnal journeys, those moments of vast silence as he wandered over the sea.

At dusk, he would cast off the moorings, and the night would begin. He would go as far as the island of Montefusco, a tiny islet off the Italian coast that was the hub of all the illegal traffic. That was where the Albanians unloaded their stolen cargoes and exchanges were made. On the return journey, his boat laden with crates of cigarettes, he would play hide-and-seek in the night with the customs boats, and this made him smile, for he knew he was the best at this game, and that no one would ever catch him.

Sometimes he would go all the way to Albania. In those cases, he would take a larger boat. But, deep down, he didn't like these long voyages. No, what he liked was to take his fishing boat and hug the coastline the way a cat hugs a wall, drifting from inlet to inlet in the sweet darkness of illegality.

He would glide over the waves in silence. Lying at the bottom of his boat, he navigated only by the stars. At those moments, he was nothing. He forgot himself. Nobody knew him anymore. Nobody spoke. He was a lost speck on the sea. A tiny wooden boat, swaying on the waves. He was nothing. Having learned to understand the language of the sea, the wind's commands, the whisper of the surf, he let the world enter him.

Smuggling was all there was. He needed the whole sky, full of wet stars, to vent his melancholy. He asked for nothing else. Only to glide with the current, leaving the world's torments behind him.

*S*omething wasn't right. It was one o'clock in the morning and Donato had berthed in the small inlet of the island of Montefusco. There was nobody under the fig tree, the spot where Raminuccio usually waited for him with the crates of cigarettes.

Raminuccio's voice rang out in the night, half-shouting, half-whispering, "Donato, over here!"

Something wasn't right. He climbed up the slope amid pebbles and prickly pears and came to the entrance of a small grotto. Raminuccio was standing there, a flashlight in hand. Behind him, two silhouettes sat on a rock, motionless and silent.

Donato gave his friend a questioning glance, and Raminuccio hastily explained.

"Don't worry. Everything's all right. I don't have any cigarettes today, but I've got something better. You'll see. For you, it makes no difference. Just drop them off at the usual place. Matteo will come pick them up. It's already arranged. Okay?"

Donato nodded. Raminuccio then stuck a fat wad of bills in his hand, whispering to him with a smile, "You'll see, it pays a lot better than cigarettes." Donato didn't count the bills, but he knew from the weight that there was at least three or four times the usual sum.

The passengers took their places in silence. Donato

didn't greet them. He began rowing away from the inlet. There was a woman of about twenty-five accompanied by her son, who must have been between eight and ten. At first Donato was entirely absorbed in his maneuver and hadn't the time to notice them, but soon the island's shore disappeared. They were out on the open sea. Donato set the motor running and had nothing better to do than to rest his eyes on his two passengers. The child was leaning his head back over his mother's knees, contemplating the night sky. The woman sat up very straight. She carried herself well. One could see from her clothing and her strong, callused hands that she was poor, but her whole face expressed an austere dignity. Donato could barely muster up the courage to speak. This feminine presence on his boat imposed a kind of new timidity on him.

"Cigarette?" he asked, holding out a pack. The woman smiled and gestured "no" with her hand. Donato immediately felt angry at himself. A cigarette. It's obvious she doesn't want one. He lit his own, thought for a moment, then spoke again, pointing his finger at himself.

"Donato. And you?"

The woman answered in a soft voice that filled the night.

"Alba."

He smiled, and repeated "Alba" several times to show that he'd understood and found the name very pretty. Then he no longer knew what to say and fell silent.

During the entire crossing, he admired the child's beautiful face and the attentive gestures of his mother, who wrapped her arms around the boy so he wouldn't catch cold. What he loved most was the woman's silence. Without knowing why, he was filled with a sort of pride. He was guiding his passengers towards the shores of the Gargano, in safety. No customs boat would ever catch them. Of all the smugglers, he was the most elusive. He felt a growing desire to stay right there, on this boat, with this woman and child. Never to reach the shore again. That night was the first time he felt this temptation. Never to go back. To stay out there among the waves. So long as the night never ended. A night as vast as a whole life, under the stars, his skin salted by sea spray. A nocturnal life, taking this woman and her son from one point to another along the clandestine coast.

The sky grew less dark. Soon the Italian coast came into view. It was four o'clock in the morning. He touched shore reluctantly. He helped the woman disembark, carried the boy, then, turning to her one last time, happy-faced, he said "*Ciao*," which for him meant a great deal more. He wanted to wish her good luck. To tell her he had loved this journey. He wanted to tell her she was beautiful, and that he loved her silence. That her son was a good boy. He wanted to tell her he wished he could see her again, that he could carry her across the sea as many times as she wanted. But all he managed to say was "*ciao*," his eyes happy and hopeful. He was sure she would understand everything that lay behind that simple word, but she merely returned his goodbye and got into the car that was waiting for her. Matteo turned off the motor and came out to say hello to Donato, leaving the two passengers seated in the back of the car.

"Everything go all right?" Matteo asked.

"Yes," Donato mumbled. He looked at Matteo and felt he could ask him the questions he hadn't had the presence of mind to ask Raminuccio. "Who are these people?"

"Illegal immigrants from Albania."

"Where are they going?"

"Here, first, then they'll be taken to Rome by truck. From there, they spread out everywhere. Germany. France. England."

"Her, too?" Donato asked, unable to make the connection between this woman and the networks Matteo was talking about.

"Pays a lot better than cigarettes, eh?" the man asked without answering his question. "They're ready to bleed themselves dry to pay for the crossing. You can almost ask whatever price you want."

He laughed, patted Donato on the shoulder, said goodbye, got back into the car and vanished with a screech of the tires.

Donato remained alone on the beach, stunned. The sun rose, monumental and slow as a sovereign. The water shimmered pink with light. He took the wad of bills out of his pocket and counted them. Two million lire. Two million lire in crumpled bills. If you added the shares of Raminuccio, Matteo, and the network boss, the

young woman must have paid at least eight million lire.*
A vast sense of shame came over Donato. He started
laughing. Howling the predatory laugh of Rocco Mascalzone. He laughed like a madman because he'd just
understood that he'd taken that woman's very last savings. He laughed, thinking, "I'm a monster. Two million
lire. I took two million lire away from her and her child.
And I was smiling at her, asking her name, thinking she
was enjoying the ride. I'm the most wretched man on
earth. To rob a woman like that, bleed her dry and then
dare to make conversation with her. I certainly am
Rocco's grandson. No faith. No shame. I'm no better
than the others. I'm even worse, a lot worse. And now
I'm rich. I have the sweat of a lifetime in my pocket, and
I'm going to celebrate at the café and buy all around. As
her boy was looking at me with those big eyes, I could
already see myself teaching him about the stars and the
sounds of the sea. Shame on me and the line of degenerates that bear my thieving name."

As of that day, Donato was never the same again. A
veil had covered his eyes, and it remained there until his
death, like a scar on his face.

onato's disappearances became more and more frequent; his journeys grew longer and longer. He was sinking into solitude without a word, without hesitation. He still saw a little of his cousin Michele, Raffaele's son, because he often slept in the small, cavelike room of the *trabucco*. Michele had a young son, Emilio Scorta. It was to him that Donato spoke his last words. When he turned eight, Donato invited him into his boat the way his uncle Giuseppe had done with him long before, and took him out for a ride to the slow rhythm of the waves. The sun set into the billows, lighting up the crests with a beautiful rosy glow. The child remained silent during the entire journey. He loved his uncle Donato very much but did not dare ask him any questions.

Finally, Donato turned to the boy and said in a soft, deep voice:

"A woman's eyes are bigger than the stars."

The child nodded without understanding. But he never forgot this statement. Donato had wanted to fulfil the Scortas' vow, to pass on a world of knowledge to one of their own. He'd thought a long time about this. He'd asked himself just what he knew and what he'd learned in life. The only thing that stood out in his mind was the night spent with Alba and her son. Alba's big, dark eyes, in which he had swum with delight. Yes, the stars had seemed tiny compared to that woman's two pupils, which hypnotized the moon itself.

The words he spoke to Emilio were Donato's last. The Scortas never saw him again. He stopped coming ashore. He was but a moving point between two shores, a boat floating into the night. He no longer transported cigarettes. He'd become a clandestine ferryman and did nothing else. Constantly passing between the Albanian and Apulian coasts, picking up and dropping off foreigners come to try their luck. Young people, thin from having eaten too little, staring at the Italian coastline with famished eyes. Young people whose hands trembled, impatient to get to work. They were about to enter a new land. They would sell their working strength to anyone who wanted it, breaking their backs picking tomatoes for the big farming concerns of Foggia or craning their necks under lamps in the illegal sweatshops of Naples. They would work like beasts, consenting to sweat out every last drop in their bodies, accepting the yoke of exploitation and the violent rule of money. They knew all this. They knew that their young bodies would be forever marked by years of labor too harsh for any human being. But they couldn't wait. And Donato would see them light up, all of them, with the same glow of voracious impatience, as the Italian coastline drew near.

The world poured into his boat, changing like the

seasons. People came to him from countries stricken by disaster. He felt as if he had his hand on the planet's pulse. He saw Albanians, Iranians, Chinese, Nigerians. They all passed through his narrow boat. He accompanied them from shore to shore, endlessly back and forth. Never was he intercepted by Italian customs agents. He would glide over the waves like a phantom vessel, demanding silence from the people he ferried, whenever he heard a motor in the distance.

Many women boarded his boat. Albanians who would find work at hotels along the coast as chambermaids or with Italian families as nurse's aides for the elderly. Nigerians who would sell their bodies along the road between Foggia and Bari, under colorful umbrellas protecting them from the sun. Iranians, drained and weary, for whom the journey had only begun, since they were going much, much farther, on to France and England. Donato gazed at all these women in silence. When one of them was traveling alone, he always managed to give her back her money before she left his boat. Every time, when the woman raised her big, astonished eyes to him, thanking him softly or even kissing his hands, he would whisper, "For Alba" and cross himself. Alba was his obsession. He had thought, at first, of asking the Albanians he ferried if they knew her, but he realized it was useless. So he remained silent, returning their bills. For Alba. For Alba, he would say. And he would think: "For Alba, from whom I took everything. For Alba, whom I left in a country that probably made her a slave." Often, the women would then stroke his cheek with their fingertips. To bless him and commend him to heaven. They would do it gently, as one does to a child, for they clearly sensed that this silent man, this taciturn runner of human cargo, was nothing more than a child who spoke to the stars.

*D*onato ended up disappearing for good. At first, Elia wasn't worried. Some fishermen friends had seen him. They'd heard him singing, as he liked to do at night, when returning from one of his secret journeys. All this proved that Donato was still around, somewhere out at sea. He was simply taking longer to come back. But weeks went by, then months, and Elia had to face the obvious. His brother had disappeared.

This disappearance left an open gash in his heart. On certain sleepless nights, he would pray that his brother hadn't been swallowed up in a storm. He couldn't bear the thought of it. He would imagine Donato's last moments amidst the raging billows. His desperate cries. He sometimes wept while imagining this wretched, lonely death, the death of the shipwrecked who can only cross themselves before the fathomless bowels of the sea.

Donato did not die in a storm. The last day of his life, he was gliding softly on the current. The waves rocked his boat without fury. The sun beat down and reflected off the vast expanse of the sea, burning the skin on his face. "How strange to be burnt up in the middle of the water," he said. "I taste salt everywhere around me. On my eyelids. On my lips. At the back of my throat.

Soon I will be a little white body, shrivelled up on the floor of my boat. The salt will have dried up my fluids and eaten my flesh. It will preserve my body the way it preserves fish in the stalls at the market. Salt-bitten, that's how I will die. But it's a slow death, and I've still got some time left. Time enough to let a little more water flow beside me."

He contemplated the shore in the distance, thinking it would still be easy for him to go back. It would require some effort, of course, because his body was weak from all the days without food. But he could still do it. Soon he would no longer be able to. Soon, even with all the willpower in the world, the coast would become an unreachable line, and the prospect of returning would become a horrible nightmare. As with a man who drowns in a few inches of water, depth meant nothing; one must have the strength to keep one's head out of the water. Soon, he would no longer be able to. For the moment, he watched the chaotic line of his homeland dance on the horizon, and it was like saying goodbye.

He cried out with all his might—not for help, but simply to see if anyone could still hear him. He cried out again. Nothing moved. Nobody answered. The landscape was unchanged. No lights came on. No boats approached. His brother's voice did not reply, not even from afar. "I'm very far away," he thought. "The world can no longer hear me. Would my brother be glad to know that I called out to him when I said goodbye to the world?"

He felt he no longer had the strength to turn back. He had just passed the threshold. Even if he had suddenly been seized by remorse, he could not have turned around. He wondered how much time would pass before he lost consciousness. Two hours? Maybe more. And after that, how long before he passed from unconsciousness into death? At nightfall, everything would speed up. But the sun was still there, protecting him. He turned the boat so that the sun was in front of him, the coast behind him, invisible. It must have been five or six o'clock in the afternoon. The sun was setting, descending into the sea, where it would vanish. It was like a road opening up in the water. He placed his boat along the axis of the sun, at the center of the path of light. All he could do was keep going. To the end. The sun was burning his mind, but he kept on talking till the end.

"On I go. A long shoal of octopi is my escort. Fish surround my boat and carry it on their scaly backs. I am leaving. The sun will show me the way. I have only to follow its heat and withstand its gaze. It has made itself less blinding for me. It recognizes me. I am one of its sons. It is waiting for me. We shall sink into the water together. Its great mane of fire will make the sea shudder. Big bubbles of steam will tell those I'm leaving that Donato is dead. I am the sun. The octopi are with me. I am the sun. To the end of the sea…"

*I*know how I will end up, don Salvatore. I've had a glimpse of what my last years will be like. I'm going to lose my mind. Don't say anything. As I've said, it's already begun. I'm going to go mad. I will confuse faces and names. Everything will become a blur. My memory will go blank and soon I won't be able to make anything out. I'll be a withered little body with no memories. An old woman with no past. I've seen this sort of thing before. When we were children, a neighbor of ours, a woman, sank into senility. She could no longer remember her son's name. She didn't even recognize him when he was standing in front of her. Everything around her disturbed her. She forgot whole portions of her life. People would find her in the streets, wandering about like a dog. She lost touch with the world around her. She lived only with her ghosts. That's what awaits me. I will forget the things around me and be with my brothers in my thoughts. My memories will fade. Fine. That's one way to go that suits me. I'll forget my own life. I'll head into death without fear or misgivings. There'll be nothing left to cry about. It'll be sweet. Forgetting will soothe my pain. I'll forget I had two sons and that one of them was taken from me. I'll forget that Donato is dead and that the sea kept his body. I'll forget everything. It'll be easier that way. I'll become like a child. Yes, that's fine with me. I'll water myself down *slowly. Die a little each day. I'll abandon Carmela Scorta without even thinking about it. The day of my death, I won't even remember who I once was. I'll no longer be sad about leaving my family; they'll be strangers to me by then.*

All I can do is wait. The sickness is inside me. Little by little, it will erase everything.

I'll never get to talk to my granddaughter. I'll die before she's old enough. Either that, or, if I hang on a little longer, I'll no longer remember what it was I wanted to tell her. There are so many things. They'll get all mixed up. I won't be able to tell any of it apart. I will babble. I will frighten her. Raffaele was right. Things need to be stated. I've told you everything. And you will tell her yourself, don Salvatore. After I'm dead or have become nothing more than an old ragdoll who can no longer talk, you will tell her for me. Anna. I'll never know the woman she'll become, but I would like for a little of myself to live on in her.

You will tell her, don Salvatore, that it's not so far-fetched to say that her grandmother was the daughter of an old Pole named Korni. You'll tell her that we chose to become the Scortas, and we huddled together to keep warm.

The wind is carrying away my words. I don't know where it will set them down. It's scattering the hills with them. But you must make sure that at least some of them reach her.

I am old, don Salvatore. I'm going to stop talking now. Thank you for coming out with me. Go home now, if you like. I'm tired. Go home. Don't worry about me. I'm going to stay a little while yet, to think about all these things one last time. Thank you, don Salvatore. And goodbye. Who knows whether I'll recognize you the next time we meet? The night is mild. It's nice out. I'm going to stay here. I would love it if the wind decided to carry me away.

IX

EARTHQUAKE

One minute earlier, nothing was happening, and life went on, slow and peaceful. One minute earlier, the tobacco shop was full, like any other day since the start of this summer of 1980. The town was packed with tourists. Whole families swelled the camping sites along the coast. During the three months of summer, the town filled up with enough money to last the whole year. The population of Montepuccio tripled. Everything changed. Girls came, beautiful and free, bringing with them the latest fashions from the North. Money flowed like water. For three months, life in Montepuccio became crazy.

One minute earlier, there was a joyous crowd of tanned bodies, elegant women, and laughing children jamming the Corso. The outdoor cafes were full. Carmela watched the uninterrupted flow of tourists. She was now an old woman with a withered body and a porous mind who spent her days in a small cane chair in front of her tobacco shop. She'd become the shadow she had predicted. Her memory had abandoned her, her mind had faltered. She was like a newborn in a wrinkled body. Elia looked after her. He'd hired a woman from town to feed her and change her clothes. Nobody could speak to her anymore. She saw the world through troubled eyes.

Everything was a threat. At times she would start groaning as though someone were twisting her wrists, her mind teeming with obscure terrors. When she felt restless, she would often wander the streets of her neighborhood, yelling her brothers' names. People had to persuade her to return home, trying patiently to calm her down. Sometimes she no longer recognized her son. More and more often, in fact. She would look right at him and say, "My son, Elia, is coming to see me." At such moments, he would clench his jaw to hold back his tears. There was nothing to be done. All the doctors he'd consulted had said so. All one could do was to keep her company along the slow road to senility. Time was gradually eating away at her and had started its feast at the head. She was nothing more than an empty body, occasionally jolted by spasms of thought. Sometimes a name or a memory would come back to her, and she would ask, in her former voice, for news about town. Had anyone thanked don Salvatore for the fruit he'd sent? How old was Anna? Elia had grown used to these flashes of false lucidity. They were merely spasms. She would always fall back into deep silence. She could no longer go any distance unaccompanied. The moment she was alone, she would get lost in the town and start crying, in that maze of narrow streets she no longer recognized.

She had never gone back to the place behind the church where the time-worn old confessional lay half-buried in the ground. She did not greet don Salvatore when she crossed him in the street. All these faces meant nothing to her. It was as though the world around her had cropped up out of thin air. She was no longer part of it. She merely sat there, on her straw chair, sometimes talking softly to herself, wringing her hands, or eating grilled almonds, given to her by her son, with a childish glee.

One minute earlier, there she was, eyes staring into space. She could hear Elia's voice inside, chatting with customers, and this voice was enough to let her know she was where she belonged.

All at once, a shudder swept over the village. People in the streets stopped dead in their tracks. A rumbling made the pavement tremble. Straight out of nowhere, but there it was. Everywhere. Like a trolley running under the asphalt. Women suddenly turned pale as they felt the ground begin to move under their light summer shoes. Something seemed to be inside the walls. Glasses tinkled in cupboards. Lamps fell on their tables. Walls rippled as though made out of paper. The Montepuccians felt as if they'd built their town on the back of an animal that was now waking up and shaking itself after centuries of slumber. Tourists looked at the natives in surprise, their incredulous eyes asking:

"What is happening?"

Then a voice in the street cried out, a voice soon echoed by dozens more: "*Terremoto! Terremoto!*"* Disbelief gave way to panic. The rumbling was vast and drowned out all other sounds. Yes, the earth was shaking, splitting the pavement, cutting the current, opening great breaches in the walls of the buildings, toppling chairs and flooding the streets with debris and dust. The earth shook with a force that it seemed nothing could temper. People were but tiny insects scurrying across the surface of the globe, praying not to be swallowed up.

But already the rumbling was subsiding, and the walls stopped trembling. People had barely the time to name the strange fury rising up from the earth before it all grew calm again. Stillness returned with the stunning simplicity of the calm after a storm. All of Montepuccio was out in the streets. By a kind of reflex, they had all left their houses and gone outside at once, fearing they might be imprisoned by debris should the walls collapse in a cloud of rubble. Now they wandered outside like sleepwalkers, looking up at the sky in a daze. Some women started crying. Children wailed. The great mass of Montepuccians didn't know what to say. They were all there, gazing at one another, happy to be alive but still quaking inside. It was no longer the earth that was rumbling under their skins, but a fear which had settled in and made their teeth chatter.

Before the streets began to echo again with shouts and cries—before everyone started counting their loved ones, before the interminable chatter of commentary and opinion on this blow of fate had begun—Elia stepped out of the tobacco shop. He'd remained inside the whole duration of the tremor. He'd had no time to think of anything, not even that he might die. He rushed into the street. His eyes ran down the sidewalk, and he started shouting, "Miuccia! Miuccia!" But nobody looked up. For at that moment, the entire Corso was awash with shouts and cries, and Elia's voice was drowned out by the din of the crowd coming back to life.

Carmela was walking slowly along the dust-covered streets. She walked on obstinately, as she hadn't done in a long time. A new strength had taken hold of her. She made her way through the groups of people, around the cracks in the pavement. She was speaking in a soft voice. Everything began to blur in her mind. The earthquake. Her brothers. Old Korni's dying moments. The past resurfaced like molten lava. She leapt from one memory to another. A crowd of faces bore down upon her. She no longer paid any attention to what was around her. Women in the street saw her pass and called to her, asking her if everything was all right, if the cataclysm hadn't destroyed anything of hers, but she didn't answer. She pressed on, stubbornly, engrossed in her thoughts. She walked up the Via dei Suplicii. It was a steep climb, and she had to stop several times to catch her breath. She took advantage of these rests to gaze down upon the town. She saw men outside in shirt-sleeves, ears to the walls, listening for possible damage. She saw children asking the question that no one could answer. Why had the earth shaken? Will it do so again? As their mothers didn't answer, she, who hadn't spoken for so long, answered for them, "Yes, the earth will shake again. The earth will shake again. Because the dead are hungry," she said in a soft voice.

Then she resumed her walk, leaving the village and
its din behind her. She reached the end of the Via dei
Suplicii, turned right onto the San Giocondo road, and
continued until she reached the gates of the cemetery.
This was where she'd wanted to go. She'd got up out of
her wooden chair with only one idea in mind: to go to
the cemetery.

The moment Carmela disappeared into the cemetery's alleys, a great silence fell over Montepuccio. As
though, all at once, every person in town had had the
same thought. One same fear gripped every heart; one
same word was on everyone's lips. "The aftershock."
Every earthquake is followed by an aftershock. There
was no getting around it. Another tremor was on its way.
It wouldn't be long now. There was no point in rejoicing
or going back home, so long as the aftershock hadn't yet
hit. So the Montepuccians huddled tightly together in
the piazza, on the Corso, on the little narrow streets.
Others went looking for blankets and a few precious
objects, in case their houses didn't withstand this second
assault.

Then they settled in for the agonizing wait for misfortune.

Elia alone kept running about, gesticulating,
plowing through the crowds, asking of all the faces he
encountered, "My mother! Has anyone seen my
mother?" Instead of answering him, they merely
repeated, "Sit down, Elia. Stay here and wait. The aftershock is coming. Stay with us." But he wouldn't listen

and continued his search, like a child lost in a crowd.

In the piazza, he heard a voice cry out, "I saw your mother! She was on the road to the cemetery." And without bothering to identify the man who had just helped him, he dashed off in that direction.

The aftershock was so sudden that it knocked Elia face down to the ground. He lay pinned to the pavement in the middle of the street. The earth roared beneath him. The stones rolled under his belly, his legs, the palms of his hands. The earth was expanding and contracting, and he could feel every one of its spasms. The rumble resonated in his bones. He stayed this way for a few seconds, face in the dust, then the tremor subsided. It was but the distant echo of a past rage. The earth, with this second warning shot, was reminding people that it existed. It was there, alive, right under their feet. Perhaps the day would come when, out of weariness or rage, it would engulf them all.

As soon as he heard the noise die down, Elia stood up. A drop of blood rolled down his cheek. The skin under one of his eyebrows had split open when he fell. Without wiping his face, he continued his race to the cemetery.

The entrance gate lay on the ground. He stepped over it and headed down the main alley. Everywhere tombstones had been ripped from the earth. Great fissures ran along the ground like scars on a sleeper's body. Statues had disintegrated. A few marble crosses lay in the grass, in pieces. The tremor had passed straight through the cemetery. It was as though a herd of mad horses had burst through the alleys, trampling on statues, upending urns and tall bouquets of dried flowers. The cemetery had collapsed like a palace built on quicksand. Elia came to a huge fissure blocking the lane. He gazed at it in silence. Here, the earth had not entirely closed back up. At that moment he realized there was no longer any point in calling out for his mother. He knew he would never see her again. The earth had swallowed her up. It would not give her back. In the warm air he could still smell his mother's perfume.

The earth had shaken and pulled Carmela's tired old body down to its innermost depths. There was nothing more to be said. He made the sign of the Cross. He stood a long time, head bowed, in the cemetery of Montepuccio, amidst the shattered vases and open graves, caressed by a warm wind that dried the blood on his cheek.

*A*nna, listen. It's old Carmela whispering to you... You don't know me... I was a senile old woman for so long, and you always kept away from me... I never talked to anyone... I didn't recognize anyone... Anna, listen. I'm going to tell you everything this time... I am Carmela Scorta... I was born several times, at different ages... First from the caress of Rocco's hand, when he ran his fingers through my hair... Then, later, from my brothers' eyes, as they gazed at me on the deck of the ship carrying us back to our wretched land... And from the shame that came over me the moment I was pulled out of the queue at Ellis Island and set apart...

The earth has split open... I know it's for me... I hear my loved ones calling me. I am not afraid... The earth has split open... I have only to step down into the crack... I will rejoin my loved ones at the center of the earth... What am I leaving behind?... Anna... I want you to hear about me... Listen, Anna, come closer... I am a failed journey to the ends of the earth... I am days of sadness at the gates of the greatest city of all... I've been furious, cowardly, and generous... I am the sun's dryness and the sea's desire.

I didn't know what to say to Raffaele, and it still makes me cry... Anna... Till the very end, all I could ever *be was the Scortas' sister... I didn't dare belong to Raf-faele... I am Carmela Scorta... I am leaving... May the earth close over me...*

X

THE PROCESSION OF SANT'ELIA

lia woke up late, his head a bit heavy. The heat had not abated during the night, and he'd had a troubled sleep. Maria prepared the espresso pot and went off to open up the tobacco shop. He got up, dull-witted, neck wet with sweat. His mind was empty of thoughts, except that today would be yet another long day. It was the feast of Sant'Elia, patron saint of Montepuccio. The cool water pouring down from the shower did him good, but no sooner did he step out, no sooner did he put on a white, short-sleeved shirt, than the heat and humidity besieged him again. It was only ten o'clock in the morning. It promised to be a stifling day.

At that hour, his small patio was in shade. He set out a wooden chair for himself to drink his coffee outside, hoping to take advantage of a slight breath of wind. He lived in a small, white, domed house with a red-tiled roof. A traditional Montepuccian house. The patio was at ground-level, jutting out onto the sidewalk but protected by a barrier. He sat down, savoring his coffee and trying to recover his senses in full.

Some children were playing in the street. Little Giuseppe, the neighbors' son, the two Mariotti brothers, and a few other kids whom Elia knew by sight. They were pretending they were killing neighborhood dogs or smiting invisible enemies. They chased one another around, shouting, grabbing each other, hiding. Suddenly a sentence stuck in his mind, something one of the kids had shouted to his companions. "We're not allowed to go any farther than the *vecchietto*."* Elia raised his head and looked down the street. The children were chasing after each other and hiding behind the fenders of cars parked along the sidewalk. Elia's eyes searched everywhere for the little old man marking the boundary of the field of play, but saw nobody. "No farther than the *vecchietto*," one of the kids repeated, shouting. Then he understood, and it made him smile. *He* was the *vecchietto*. There, in his chair, he was the little old man who served as the boundary for the racecourse. Then his mind strayed, and he forgot the little boys, their cries and imaginary gunshots. He remembered how his uncles themselves had once sat in front of their houses, just as he was doing now. At the time, they had seemed old to him. He remembered how his mother, before dying, used to sit in this same cane chair and spend whole afternoons contemplating the neighborhood's streets, letting their sounds fill her ears. Now it was his turn. He was old. A whole life had gone by. His daughter was twenty. Anna. A daughter he never tired of contemplating. Yes, time had passed. Now it was his turn to sit in cane chairs on street corners, watching the young hurry past.

Had he been happy? He thought back on all the years gone by. How to weigh a man's life? His had been like anyone else's. Full, by turns, of joy and tears. He'd lost his loved ones. His uncles, his mother, his brother. He'd known that sorrow. Felt abandoned and useless. Yet he'd kept intact the joy of having Maria and Anna beside him, and that redeemed everything. Had he been happy? He thought back on the years that had followed the fire and his marriage. It all seemed so remote now, like someone else's life. He thought back on those years, and it seemed to him as if he hadn't had a second to catch his breath. He was always running after money. He'd worked until his nights became no longer than his siestas. But, yes, he'd been happy. His uncle was right. Old *zio Faelucc'* was right when he said one day, "Make the most of your sweat." That was what he'd done. He'd been happy and exhausted. His happiness was born of fatigue. He had struggled. Fought hard. And now that he'd become this little old man sitting in his chair, now that he'd succeeded in rebuilding his business, in giving his wife and daughter a comfortable life, now that he was finally safe, out of poverty's reach, he no longer felt that keen sense of happiness. He lived in comfort and peace, which was already lucky. He had money. Yet that wild happiness, the kind one must wrest from life, that was behind him.

Little Giuseppe was called home by his mother. Elia was roused from his thoughts by the warm and potent sound of that maternal voice. He looked up. The kids had vanished like a cloud of grasshoppers. He stood up. The day was about to begin. It was Sant'Elia's day today. It was hot, and he had a lot of things to do.

*H*e went out and walked up the Corso. The town had changed. He tried to remember what it had been like fifty years earlier. How many businesses that he'd known as a child were still there? Slowly, everything had been transformed. The sons had taken over their fathers' affairs. The signs had changed. The outdoor cafés were bigger.

Elia walked down streets decked out for the celebration. This, in fact, was the only thing that hadn't changed. Today, as yesterday, the townsfolk's passion lit up the façades. Garlands of electric light bulbs hung from one sidewalk to the other. He passed a candy vendor's stand. Two huge carts full of caramels, licorice, lollipops, and every manner of sweets turned all the children's heads. A bit further on, a peasant's son offered kids rides on the back of his mule, tirelessly walking up and down the Corso. The children would cling to the animal, apprehensively at first, then beg their parents to buy them another ride. Elia stopped. He thought back on old Muratti, his uncles' smoking donkey. How many times had they climbed onto his back, he and his brother Donato, with the joy of conquerors? How many times had they begged *zio* Mimì or *zio* Peppe to let them take a ride? They adored that old donkey. They used to shriek with laughter watching him smoke his long stalks of wheat. And when the old beast, a surly, mischievous glint in his eye, would spit out the butt with the nonchalance of an old desert camel, they would raucously applaud. They just loved that old donkey. Muratti died of lung cancer—which in the end proved, to unbelievers, that he really did smoke, inhaling just like a human. If the old beast had lived longer, Elia would have pampered him tenderly. His daughter would have loved him. He could imagine Anna as a little girl, bursting out laughing at the sight of the old burro. He would have taken his daughter for rides on the animal's back through the streets of Montepuccio, and the neighborhood children would have been speechless. But Muratti was dead. He belonged to a past that only Elia seemed to remember. Tears came to his eyes. Not for the donkey, but because he had thought again of his brother, Donato. He remembered the strange, silent boy who used to take part in all his games and knew all his secrets. Yes, he had once had a brother. Donato was the only person to whom Elia could talk about his childhood and know he would be understood. The scent of dried tomatoes at *zia* Mattea's house. *Zia* Maria's stuffed eggplant. The stone-throwing brawls with the boys from nearby neighborhoods. Donato, like him, had lived through it all. He could remember those distant years with the same precision and nostalgia as Elia did. But today Elia was alone. Donato had never come back, and his disappearance had etched two long wrinkles under Elia's eyes. The wrinkles of a brother who had lost his brother.

The humidity made one's skin sticky. There wasn't a breath of wind to dry the body's sweat. Elia walked slowly, so as not to soak his shirt, taking care to hug the walls in shade. He arrived before the great white gate of the cemetery and went inside.

At that hour, on the patron saint's feast day, there was nobody around. The old women had got up early to put flowers on their late lamented husbands' graves. It was all empty and silent.

He went down the lanes, surrounded by sunstruck white marble. He walked slowly, squinting to read the names of the dead etched in stone. All the families of Montepuccio were there. The Tavagliones, the Biscottis, the Espositos, the De Nittis. Fathers and sons, cousins and aunts. Everyone. Whole generations, co-existing in a garden of marble.

"I know more people here than in town," Elia said to himself. "Those kids this morning were right. I'm a little old man. My loved ones are almost all here. I guess that's how you can tell that the years have caught up with you."

He found an odd sort of comfort in this idea. He was less afraid of dying when he thought of all those who had made the transition before him. Like a child who trembles in front of a ditch he must cross, but who, when he sees his friends jump and cross over to the other side, grows bold and thinks to himself: "If they can do it, so can I." That's exactly what he told himself. If all those others had died—and they were no braver or tougher than he—then he himself could die in turn.

He now approached the area where his family lay buried. Every one of his uncles had been interred with his wife. There wasn't a vault big enough to hold all the Scortas. But they'd specifically requested not to be put too far away from one another. Elia took a few steps back and sat down on a bench. From where he was sitting, he could see them all. Uncle Mimì *vaffanculo*. Uncle Peppe *pancia piena*. Uncle Faelucc'. He sat there a long time, under the sun, forgetting the heat, paying no attention to the sweat running down his back. He thought of his uncles, and what they had meant to him. He thought of the stories they had told him. He had loved those three men with all his childish heart. More than his own father, who had often seemed like a stranger to him, uneasy at family reunions, unable to pass on a bit of himself to his sons. Whereas the three uncles, for their part, were forever looking after him and Donato, with the generosity of mature, somewhat world-weary men towards new and innocent children. He couldn't begin to compile an exhaustive list of everything he'd gotten from them. Words. Gestures. Values, too. He realized this now that he was a father and his grown-up daughter sometimes chided him for his ways of thinking, which she said were outdated. Such as never talking about money. Giving one's word of honor.

Being hospitable. Bearing grudges. He got all this from his uncles, and he knew it.

Elia sat there on his bench, letting thoughts merge with memories, a smile on his lips, surrounded by cats that seemed to have come up out of the earth. Was the heat of the sun, beating straight down on him, making him hallucinate? Or were the vaults really letting some of their tenants out for a brief moment? His vision seemed to blur, and then he saw his uncles right there, barely two hundred yards away. He saw Domenico, Giuseppe, and Raffaele, all sitting around a wooden table, playing cards, as they loved to do, on the Corso in the late afternoon. He was dumbfounded and didn't move. He could see them so clearly. They'd aged a little, perhaps, but barely. Each still had the same tics, the same gestures, the same profile. They were laughing. The cemetery belonged to them. And the empty lanes echoed with the sweet sound of cards being slapped down on the table.

Sitting slightly apart from the table was Carmela. She was watching the card game, berating one of her brothers when he made a bad move, or defending the one that the others ganged up on.

A drop of sweat ran down from Elia's eyebrows and made him close his eyes. He became aware that the sun was beating down hard. He stood up and, without taking his eyes off his loved ones, he withdrew, walking backwards. Soon he could no longer hear their conversation.

He crossed himself and commended their souls to God, humbly begging Him to let them play cards until the end of time.

Then he turned around and left.

*H*e felt an overwhelming desire to talk to don Salvatore. Not as parishioner to village priest— Elia seldom went to church—but man to man. The old Calabrian was still alive, keeping the slow rhythms of old age. A new priest had arrived in Montepuccio, a young man from Bari named don Lino, whom the women liked. They adored him, in fact, and were forever saying that it was time Montepuccio had a modern priest who understood the problems of the day and knew how to speak to the young. And don Lino did know how to touch young people's hearts. He became their confidant. He played guitar late into the night at parties on the beach in summer. He reassured the town's mothers, savored their pies, and listened to their marital problems with a smile full of restraint and concentration. Montepuccio was very proud of its new priest. All of Montepuccio, in fact, except for the old folks, who saw him only as a flirt. What they'd liked most about don Salvatore was his frankness and peasantlike roughness; to them, the *Barese** was not of the same mettle as his predecessor.

Don Salvatore had refused to leave Montepuccio. He wanted to live out his last days there, among his flock, in his church. It was impossible to tell how old the Calabrian priest was. He was an old man with wiry muscles and a harrier's gaze. He was getting on towards eighty, and time seemed to have forgotten him. Death would not come.

Elia found him in his little garden, feet in the grass and a cup of coffee in hand. Don Salvatore invited him to sit down beside him. The two men loved each other deeply. They chatted a bit, then Elia opened up to his friend and told him what was tormenting him.

"The generations follow one after the other, don Salvatore. But what does it mean, when all is said and done? Do we get anywhere in the end? Look at my family, the Scortas. Each one fought hard, in his way, and each, in his way, managed to outdo himself. To get where? To me? Am I really any better than my uncles were? No. So what was the purpose of all their effort? There wasn't any, don Salvatore. There wasn't any. It's enough to make you cry."

"Yes," replied don Salvatore, "the generations follow one after the other. One simply has to do one's best, pass things on, and make way for the others."

Elia remained silent a moment. He liked the priest's way of not trying to simplify problems or give them a positive turn. Many churchmen have that flaw. They sell heaven to their flocks, which leads them to make silly speeches about cheap consolation. Not don Salvatore. It was enough to make you think his faith was no consolation whatsoever to him.

"I was just asking myself," the priest continued, "before you arrived, what the town had become. It's the same problem, on a different scale. You tell me, Elia: what has Montepuccio become?"

"A bag of money on a pile of stones," Elia said bitterly.

"Right. Money has driven them mad. With the desire to have it, and the fear of not having any. Money is their sole obsession."

"Maybe so," Elia replied, "but you have to admit that the Montepuccians aren't starving to death anymore. Children no longer get malaria, and all the houses have running water."

"Yes," said don Salvatore, "we've grown rich, but who will ever measure the impoverishment that has gone hand-in-hand with this evolution? The town's life is poor. These fools haven't even realized it."

Elia thought don Salvatore was exaggerating, but then he thought of how his uncles had lived, and what his uncles had done for one another. Had Elia done the same for his brother Donato?

"Now it's our turn to die, Elia," the priest said gently.

"Yes," said Elia, "my life is behind me. A life of ciga-rettes. All those cigarettes sold, adding up to nothing. Just hot air and smoke. My mother sweated, my wife and I sweated over those packs of dried leaves that vanished between our customers' lips. Tobacco gone up in smoke, that's what my life has been. Clouds of smoke disap-pearing in the wind. It all adds up to nothing. Just a strange life that people puffed on nervously or inhaled in long, calm drags on summer nights."

"Don't worry. I'll go before you do. You still have a little time left."

"Yeah."

"What a shame," the priest added. "I loved them so much, these bumpkins of mine. I can't bring myself to leave them."

Elia smiled. He found this remark very odd on the lips of a churchman. What about eternal rest and the joy of being called to sit at God's right hand? He wanted to point out this contradiction to his friend, but he didn't dare.

"Sometimes I think you're not really a priest," he merely said, smiling.

"I haven't always been one."

"What about now?"

"Right now, I'm thinking about life, and I feel furious that I have to leave it behind. I'm thinking about the Lord, and the thought of His goodness isn't enough to ease my pain. I think I've loved people too much to resign myself to abandoning them. If I could just know for certain that, from time to time, I would receive news of Montepuccio."

"It's time to pass things on," said Elia, repeating the priest's words.

"Yes." Silence fell over the two men. Then don Salvatore's face lit up and he added: "Olives are eternal. One olive doesn't last. It ripens and then it spoils. But the olives keep growing, over and over, forever. They are all different, but their long chain of succession never ends. They all have the same shape, the same color; they ripen under the same sun and have the same taste. So, yes, olives are eternal. Like people. It's the same unending succession of life and death. The long chain of mankind will not break. Soon it will be my turn to pass away. Life is drawing to a close. But it will continue for everyone else."

The two men remained silent. Then Elia realized he was going to be late to the tobacco shop, and took leave of his old friend. As he warmly shook his hand, it seemed to him that don Salvatore was about to add something. But he didn't, and the two men parted.

"What on earth is she doing?"

Elia was now standing in the doorway of the tobacco shop. The evening sun caressed the facades along the street. It was eight o'clock, and for Elia, it was a sacred moment. The lights of the town were on. A dark crowd crammed the sidewalks of the Corso. A motionless, noisy crowd. The procession was about to pass, and Elia wanted to be there, in front of his shop, to see it. As he had always done. And as his mother, before him, had done. He waited. The throng began to crowd around him.

"What on earth is she doing?"

He was waiting for his daughter. He had told her that morning, "Come to the shop for the procession." And as she had said yes without seeming really to have heard him, he'd repeated twice: "Eight o'clock in front of the shop. Don't forget." She had laughed, stroked his cheek, and chided him, saying, "Yes, papa, just like every year. I won't forget."

The procession was about to pass and she wasn't there. Elia started fretting. It wasn't such a complicated matter, after all. The town wasn't so big that you could get lost in it. Too bad. If she wasn't there, it was because she hadn't understood a thing. He would watch the procession all by himself. Anna was a beautiful girl. She'd left Montepuccio at the age of eighteen to study medicine in Bologna, a long course of study that she'd begun with enthusiasm. It was Elia who'd pressed her to choose Bologna. The girl could have easily imagined herself in Naples, but Elia wanted the best for his daughter and had misgivings about life in Naples. She was the first of the Scortas to leave the village and try her luck up North. There was never any question of her taking over the tobacco shop. Elia and Maria were dead set against it, and in any case, their daughter had no desire to do so. For the moment, she was utterly thrilled to be a student in a beautiful university city full of boys with sparkling eyes. She was discovering the world, and Elia was proud of this. His daughter was doing what he himself hadn't done when *zio* Domenico had suggested it to him. She was the first to extricate herself from this dry land that had nothing to offer. She was probably leaving forever. Elia and Maria had often talked about this. It was quite possible she would meet a boy, decide to settle there, perhaps get married. She would soon become one of those beautiful, elegant women covered with jewelry who come to spend one month a year, in summer, on the beaches of the Gargano.

He was thinking of all this, standing motionless on the sidewalk, when, at the corner of the street, he saw the great banner of Sant'Elia appear, swaying slowly, hypnotically, over the passersby. The procession was arriving. At its head, a lone man, strong and sturdy, was carrying a wooden pole from which hung a long banner with the town's colors. He proceeded slowly, weighed down by the heavy velvet fabric and taking care not to let the pole get caught among the electric lights hanging from the lampposts. Behind him the procession came into view. Elia stiffened, straightened the collar of his shirt, put his hands behind his back, and waited. He was about to grumble about his daughter already being a perfect Milanese, when he felt a young, nervous hand slip into his own. He turned around. There was Anna. Smiling. He looked at her. She was a beautiful woman, with all the carefree joy of her years. Elia kissed her and made room for her beside him, keeping her hand in his.

Anna was late because don Salvatore had taken her to the old confessional. He'd talked to her for several hours and told her everything, and it was as though Carmela's old, cracking voice were caressing the grass on the hillsides. The image that Anna had retained of her grandmother—a senile old woman with a weary, ugly body—had been swept away as Carmela spoke through the priest's mouth. Henceforth, Anna would carry the secrets of New York and Raffaele inside her. She was determined to say nothing to her father. She didn't want New York to be taken away from the Scortas. Without her really knowing why, these secrets made her feel strong, infinitely strong.

The procession paused for a moment. Everything came to a standstill. The crowd fell silent, collecting itself, and then the march resumed to the shrill and powerful sounds of the brass section. The procession's passing was a moment of grace. Music filled people's souls. Elia felt part of a whole. The statue of Sant'Elia drew near, carried by eight men covered in sweat. It seemed to dance above the crowd, gently swaying like a ship on the waves, rolling to the rhythms of the men's steps. The Montepuccians made the sign of the Cross as it passed, and, at that moment, Elia's and don Salvatore's eyes met. The old priest nodded at him, smiled for emphasis, then blessed him. Elia thought of the time long ago when he had stolen the medals of San Michele and the whole village had hunted for him to make him pay for his blasphemous act. He crossed himself with feeling, letting the warmth of the old priest's smile permeate him.

When the saint's statue was in front of the tobacco shop, Anna squeezed her father's hand a little tighter, and Elia felt that he'd been mistaken. His daughter might be the first to leave the village, but she was a Montepuccian through and through. She belonged to this land. She had its eyes and its pride. At that moment, she whispered in his ear: "Nothing ever satisfies the Scortas." Elia said nothing. He was surprised by her comment, and especially by the calm, decisive tone in which she'd uttered it. What did she mean? Was she trying to warn him about some family shortcoming she'd just discovered? Or to tell him that she was familiar with and shared the Scorta's ancient hunger, the hunger that had been their strength and their curse? He thought of all this, and suddenly it occurred to him that the meaning of her statement was much simpler than that. Anna was a Scorta. She had just become one. Despite the Manuzio name that she bore. Yes, that was it. She had just chosen the Scortas. He looked at her. Her gaze was deep and beautiful. Anna, the last of the Scortas. She had chosen the name. Chosen the line of the sun-eaters. She would make their insatiable appetite her own. Nothing ever satisfies the Scortas. With their eternal desire to eat the sky and drink the stars. He wanted to say something in response, but suddenly the music resumed, drowning out the murmurs of the crowd. He said nothing. He squeezed his daughter's hand tightly.

Maria joined them in the doorway of the shop. She too had aged, but her eyes still had that wild glimmer that had driven Elia crazy. They huddled closely together, surrounded by the crowd. A powerful feeling swept over them. The procession was right in front of them. Its powerful music exhilarated them. The whole town was there. Children with candies in their hands. Women wearing perfume. It was as though it had always been this way. They stood quite erect in front of their tobacco shop. Proudly. Not with the arrogant pride of upstarts, but proud simply because the moment felt right.

Elia crossed himself and kissed the medal of the Blessed Virgin, a gift from his mother, that he wore around his neck. His place was here. There was no doubt about it. His place was here, in front of the tobacco shop. It could not be otherwise. He thought back on that eternity of actions, prayers, and hopes, and took great comfort in it. He had been a man, he thought to himself. Just a man. And all was well. Don Salvatore was right. Mankind, under the sun of Montepuccio, was, like the olives, eternal.

AUTHOR'S POSTSCRIPT

As I finish this book, my thoughts go out to all those people who, by opening the doors to these lands for me, made it possible for me to write it. My parents, who passed on to me their love of Italy. Alexandra, who led me to discover the South of the peninsula and afforded me the pleasure and honor of seeing it through her loving, sunlit eyes. Renato, Franca, Nonna Miuccia, Zia Sina, Zia Graziella, Domenico, Carmela, Lino, Mariella, Antonio, Federica, Emilia, Antonio, and Angelo, for their hospitality and warmth; the stories they told me; the dishes they allowed me to savor; the hours spent in their company on fragrant summer days; and for what they conveyed to me, without even realizing, about a way of belonging to life that I find only in these lands and which always overwhelms me. I hope they will all recognize a bit of themselves in these pages. It would only be right, since they were there with me during all those hours as I struggled alone with each page. These lines were written for them. My only wish is that my words express how precious those moments under the Apulian sun were to me.

NOTES

p. 5. the Gargano massif: A rocky massif in the region of Apulia in southeastern Italy.

p. 13. *la mala vita*: (It.) Literally, "the bad life." In modern times (written as a single word, *malavita*), it has also become synonymous with the criminal underworld.

p. 13. *carabinieri*: The national police force in Italy, as distinguished from, for example, the local police forces. The carabinieri are a branch of the army.

p. 42. Faelucc': Pronounced *fie-LOOCH*. Shortened version of Raffaeluccio, diminutive of Raffaele.

p. 45. the Corso: The Corso is usually the main street in an Italian town or city, though large urban centers may have more than one Corso. Rome, for example, has several, including the Via del Corso (usually called "il corso") and the Corso Vittorio Emanuele, two of the main arteries in the city's center.

p. 65. *Ma vaffanculo!*: A common Italian obscenity, roughly the equivalent of "go fuck yourself" (literally, "go bugger yourself").

p. 67. *pancia piena*: (It.) "full belly."

p. 67. *Madonna, che pasta!*: (It.) "My, what good pasta!"

p. 67. *sugo*: (It.) sauce.

p. 84. Spaccanapoli: An ancient, central quarter of Naples containing many of its most famous monuments and typically narrow streets. It is named after the equally ancient street that slices through the city, splitting it, as it were, in two (*spaccare* means "to split" or "to break").

p. 105. *passeggiata*: (It.) "Stroll" or "promenade." The evening *passeggiata*, when nearly everyone in town comes out to socialize, is an age-old custom in Italian towns large and small.

p. 108. State Monopolies: Tobacco, like salt, is a government-controlled product in Italy, overseen by the Monopolio di Stato.

p. 108. *caciocavallo … limoncello*: Caciocavallo is a pear-shaped cheese typical of Apulia and all of Southern Italy; limoncello is a lemon liqueur, also southern, usually served very chilled.

p. 109. *Tabaccheria Scorta Mascalzone Rivendita no. 1*: "Scorta Mascalzone Tobacconist, Store no. 1."

p. 123-4. *È arrivato l'asino fumatore! L'asino fumatore!*: (It.) "It's the smoking donkey! The smoking donkey!"

p. 124. Muratti: *Muratti Ambassador* is a brand of Italian cigarettes, once considered "high-class."

p. 173. *amore di zio*: (It.) Literally, "love of your uncle," a term of endearment for one's nephew.

p. 180. *fra*: (It.) An affectionate abbrevation of the word *fratello*, "brother."

p. 206. "*Aïe, aïe, aïe / Domani non mi importa per niente / Questa notte devi morire con me*": (It.) "Ah, ah, ah!/ Tomorrow means nothing to me / Tonight you must die with me." [Footnoted in original text.]

p. 227. eight million lire: At the time this episode is occurring, this would have been worth about eight thousand dollars.

p. 245. *Terremoto! Terremoto!*: (It.) "Earthquake! Earthquake!"

p. 260. *vecchietto*: (It.) "Little old man."

p. 269. *Barese*: (It.) Someone from the Apulian city of Bari.

ABOUT THE TRANSLATORS

Stephen Sartarelli is an award-winning translator and poet. His most recent volume of verse is *The Open Vault* (Spuyten Duyvil, 2001).

Sophie Hawkes is a painter and printmaker and has translated widely from the French. They live together in southwest France.